Bridget sat next to Cody on the bed, and he sent her an excited smile.

"Dad is so awesome, Mom. You were wrong about him. He's not the same as your dad."

"I'm glad you like him." But she'd expected as much. Cody already had been building a preconceived notion of the hero his father was going to be, and all Bridget could do was keep hoping and praying that Kade didn't let him down.

"Did he tell you what my present is?"

"No, he didn't."

"Do you think he'll bring me something every time he visits?"

"I don't know. But this isn't about getting gifts."

"I know. I was just asking what you thought. I asked him if he still likes you, and he said he still thinks you're sweet and pretty. He wants to be friends with you again."

She wished Cody hadn't brought her into it. She was already feeling the heat of being near Kade, of being far too attracted to him...

* * *

FAMILY RENEWAL:
Sometimes all it takes is a second chance

Dear Reader,

What words would you use to describe book-hero cowboys? Romantic? Chivalrous? Sexy? Kind? Loving? Daring? Charming? Brooding? I can think of all sorts of descriptions, depending on the man himself.

The cowboy in this story is Kade Quinn, a successful horse trainer and loner who travels for his work and has no interest in putting down roots. Of course, his life is going to change when he discovers that he has a ten-year-old son with a beautiful woman from his past.

Along with the cowboy theme, this story also has significant references to floriography and the language of flowers. In the Victorian era, people would send each other bouquets in which each plant and flower had a meaning. I have always been fascinated by this and thought it would be fun to incorporate it into some of my Harlequin books.

If you read *The Bachelor's Baby Dilemma*, my previous Family Renewal book, you'll remember that it had floriography references, too. For *Coming Home to a Cowboy*, I'm sending all of you an imaginary bouquet that represents the title and contents of the story.

Azalea (romance)
Daffodil (chivalry)
Lilac (the first emotions of love)
Tulip (the perfect lover)
Forget-Me-Not (true love)
Rose, white (love, beauty, unity)
Carnation, light red (fascination)
Rose, deep red (passion)

I could include many, many more, but for now, I'll stop there. Just remember, though, that if you make up your own language-of-flowers bouquets, there are different meanings to some of the same flowers, depending on which dictionary you use. It's a wondrous and complex language.

Best wishes (basil),

Sheri WhiteFeather

Coming Home to a Cowboy

———

Sheri WhiteFeather

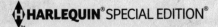

HARLEQUIN® SPECIAL EDITION®

ISBN-13: 978-0-373-65911-1

Coming Home to a Cowboy

Copyright © 2015 by Sheree Henry-Whitefeather

Printed in U.S.A.

www.Harlequin.com

Sheri WhiteFeather is an award-winning, bestselling author. She writes a variety of romance novels for Harlequin and has become known for incorporating Native American elements into her stories. She has two grown children who are tribally enrolled members of the Muscogee Creek Nation. She lives in California and enjoys shopping in vintage stores and visiting art galleries and museums. Sheri loves to hear from her readers at sheriwhitefeather.com.

Books by Sheri WhiteFeather

Harlequin Special Edition

Family Renewal

The Bachelor's Baby Dilemma
Lost and Found Husband
Lost and Found Father

Byrds of a Feather

The Texan's Future Bride

Silhouette Romantic Suspense

Imminent Affair
Protecting Their Baby

Silhouette Desire

Marriage of Revenge
The Morning-After Proposal

Visit the Author Profile page at Harlequin.com for more titles.

Chapter One

Kade Quinn went into shocked silence, his cell phone pressed to his ear. He had no idea what he was supposed to say to Bridget Wells, the woman on the other end of the line. Not after she'd just told him that he was the father of her ten-year-old son.

He couldn't deny that he'd had a fling with her that fit the timeline, but conceiving a child with her wasn't in his realm of comprehension.

Struggling to process the information, he let out the breath he'd been holding. In the background, the horses he was training were nickering for his attention. But he couldn't focus on them right now. Bridget's news was the only thing he could think about, along with the incessant pounding of his frantic heart.

"I don't understand," he finally said. "If you've known all along that he's mine, then why are you just telling me now?"

"Cody decided that he wants to meet you." She spoke quietly, nervously, it seemed. "He's the one who looked up your website and got your current phone number."

Kade remained beyond nervous, too. "Cody? That's his name?"

"Yes."

"How long has he known that I'm his dad?"

"For most of his life. But he accepted not meeting you until now. My grandfather helped raise me, and he helped raise my son, too. Grandpa was Cody's role model, his father figure of sorts. But then Grandpa died last year, leaving Cody lonely for paternal companionship." After a slight pause, she said, "Not that I expect you to…"

Step up to the plate? Be the boy's new role model? "If that isn't what you're expecting, then why did you call me?"

"Because I promised Cody that I would."

So what did that mean? That Kade could refuse to meet his son? That he could walk away unscathed?

There was no way in hell that he could ever do that. Kade had issues with his own father, a man he hadn't spoken to in years. He would never willingly mimic his old man's behavior. "You should have told me you were pregnant. You should have called me back then."

"I made what I thought was the right decision at the time, given the circumstances. So please don't fault me for that."

He frowned, troubled by her reluctance to include him in Cody's life. She still sounded leery. "What circumstances?"

"You never kept in touch, Kade. You never even

called me after you left, even though you said that you would."

"I know, but time just got away from me. Besides, I'm bad about that kind of stuff."

Her breath rushed out. "That's just my point."

He struggled to follow her logic. "So because I didn't call you, you didn't call me? Even after you found out that you were pregnant?"

"Truthfully, it's more complicated than that. But I don't want to discuss it over the phone. If you're going to come to Montana and meet Cody, we can talk about it then."

"Are you still in the same area?"

"Yes. In Flower River."

His thoughts drifted back to the past. Bridget had attended one of his training clinics at the fairgrounds in the town where she lived. He'd been intrigued from the start, noticing her that very first day. She'd been his physical ideal: a blue-eyed blonde with a curvy figure that turned him on. Mostly, though, she was just a sweet, no-frills girl who'd never even been out of Montana.

They'd embarked on a weeklong tryst, and being with her was the most fun he'd ever had with anyone. It wasn't just about the heat that unfolded between the sheets, but the compatibility when they were hanging out together.

For Kade, that was a rare occurrence. A loner by nature, he preferred to keep to himself. He could count the number of women he'd been with on one hand. Okay, maybe two. But he could go for years at a time without partaking of anyone's company. Sometimes he missed the warmth of a woman's body next to his. But it was easier to stay unattached than get pulled into romantic entanglements.

A week, he supposed, was his limit. The precise amount of time he'd spent with the mother of his child.

He squinted into the sun. "Did I make that bad of an impression on you, Bridget?"

"What?" she replied.

"For you to have left me out of Cody's life."

"I already told you that it's complicated." She cleared her throat. "Just tell me if you want to meet Cody, and we'll go from there. But if you have reservations, then please stay away. It has to be something you can handle. Otherwise Cody could end up getting hurt."

"Of course I want to meet him." He couldn't just ignore the fact that he had a son. He wanted to do the right thing, to take responsibility, to make a difference in the kid's life. "And I'm not going to hurt him, not if I can help it. I got hurt plenty by my own dad. I know what that feels like."

"Really? I didn't know you had a troubled relationship with your father."

"It's not something I normally talk about."

"I had a problem with my dad, too."

A bell went off in his head. "Is that part of the complication you keep mentioning?"

"Yes." Her voice broke a little. "And I was just protecting Cody from more of the same. But like I said, we can talk about that when you're able to come here."

He didn't doubt that it was a long and painful story. But he was still concerned about the specifics and how it applied to him. "I can rearrange things so I can be free sometime next week. But I'm going to drive, not fly, so that'll add a few more days."

"Where are you right now?"

"In Texas." He glanced around the Heartbreak Paint Ranch, a high-end facility that belonged to one of his clients, a country singer and his fashion-model wife. "I'm on a job. I travel the way I always did, and I still do clinics. But I also work for a lot of private parties now. I've come a long way since you knew me."

"I'm aware of the reputation you've built for yourself. Cody scoured your webpage. He's impressed by the famous people you know and all the flashy horses you train. Ever since he got it in his head to meet you, you're all he's been talking about. He's even been bragging about you to his friends."

Kade hoped he could live up to those kinds of expectations. "I'll do my best to make him proud."

"Thank you. He's going to be thrilled." Her voice went soft. "After we hang up, I can email you some pictures of him."

"That would be great." Kade couldn't even begin to imagine what his son looked like. "Can I ask you something personal? Since you said that your grandfather was Cody's father figure, does that mean that you've never been married or had a significant other who influenced him?"

"No, there's been no one. No one important," she clarified. "I'm careful about the men I date and whom I let Cody get close to."

Kade figured as much, being that he'd also been left out of the loop. Nonetheless, he was glad that there wasn't an ex-husband or some other dude who'd once mattered. He didn't want to be compared with anyone else. It was scary enough that Cody was already putting him on a pedestal.

She said, "I'll email you those pictures, and once you work out your schedule, you can let me know for certain what day you'll be here."

"Sure. Okay." Curious about her appearance and how much she might've changed, he wanted to ask her to send a picture of herself, too, but he thought that might seem weird. He would be seeing her in person soon enough. "Tell Cody I said hello, and I'm looking forward to meeting him."

"I will. Bye for now."

"Bye." He pushed the end button and stared into space, unsure of what to do next. Should he call his brother in California and tell him the news? Yes, he should. But he decided he would do that after he saw Cody's pictures.

For now, he opted for checking his emails on his phone, hoping Bridget had hurried and sent them.

She hadn't, at least not yet.

He kept checking, and about ten minutes later, the email arrived with a subject line that read "Cody Colton Wells."

So that was his son's full name? He liked the sound of it, but he would have preferred that the boy's surname was Quinn instead of Wells. At least that would've made Kade feel more like Cody's father, not left out of everything.

He opened the attached files, and talk about being knocked off his feet. The first image appeared to be a school picture, where Cody was looking straight at the camera with a posed expression. Kade saw himself in the boy: his deep-set eyes, his naturally tanned complexion, even the cowlick in the front of his short dark hair. Kade's was in a different spot and not quite as pronounced, but he still had one.

The next picture was much more casual, with Cody sitting on the porch of a little blue-and-white house that was positioned on a dirt road and surrounded by trees.

Was that Bridget's house? The place where she was raising Cody? When Kade and Bridget were together, she'd stayed with him at the motel room he'd rented for the week. He hadn't gone home with her because she'd still lived with her family then. It would have been awkward for her to bring him there or introduce him to anyone.

But this time would be different. Kade would be going straight to her door—nearly eleven years later—to meet the child they'd created.

Before he panicked from the sheer craziness of it, he opened the third and final photo, which showed Cody by a Christmas tree in the midst of holiday hoopla, wrapping paper everywhere. Again, Cody looked just like Kade when he got dressed up, with a crisp Western shirt and bolo tie.

Should he reply to Bridget's email? Should he tell her what a handsome kid they had? Or would that sound arrogant, given Cody's resemblance to him? He smiled, feeling ridiculously proud that his genes were so strong.

Even if he still didn't know a damned thing about being a father.

Bridget was a nervous wreck, her pulse pounding beneath her skin. Kade was scheduled to arrive today.

For now, Cody was at school. She and Kade had agreed to see each other first, to talk, to get the past out of the way before their son got home.

Their son. Hers and Kade's.

The week they'd spent together had been the most beautiful, romantic time of her life. She'd relived every passionate moment after he was gone, waiting by the phone for him to call, just as Bridget's mom had routinely done with Bridget's dad. Two women, generations apart, infatuated with the same type of men. Lessons, she thought, learned the hard way.

Struggling to clear her mind, to temper her regret over her family history, she glanced at the kitchen clock. Since Kade would be there during lunchtime, she'd made a beef stew that was simmering in a slow cooker, just in case he was hungry.

Fool that she was, Bridget went into her room to check her appearance for the gazillionth time. Normally she wasn't the fussy sort. But today she was wearing her best jeans and nicest blouse. Her hair was long and loose, instead of pulled back in a ponytail or plaited into a single braid. She'd even resorted to a little mascara and lip gloss. Cody had told her that she looked "purty" this morning, and for her that went a long way.

He was so darned excited when he'd gone off to school, chattering about the anticipation of meeting his dad. He'd even printed Kade's bio from his website and stuck it in his notebook so he could study it again at recess.

Her baby boy had a serious case of idol worship. Once upon a time, Bridget had felt that way about her father, too.

Trying to get a grip on her emotions, she returned to the kitchen and waited for Kade to show up. At least she'd seen pictures of him on the internet so she knew what to expect in that regard. As far as she could tell, he was still as hot as sin, with the same piercing brown eyes, granite-cut jaw and striking cheekbones.

The instant the doorbell rang, she dashed off to answer it. She opened the door, and there he was. All man. All six foot four inches of solid muscle. His hair was combed straight back, the ends skimming his collar, and his clothes consisted of timeworn denim. Seeing him in person was far more breathtaking than viewing a picture could ever be. He'd aged, of course, going from his midtwenties to midthirties, but it looked incredibly fine on him.

Bridget was in her thirties, too. Thirty-one, in fact, with a birthday that had just passed.

"Hello," he said, shooting her a smile she remembered from long ago.

"Hi," she replied, warning her heart to be still. A dizzying moment later, he leaned in for a hug.

Dang, he moved fast. She would have preferred a less intimate greeting. But she put her arms around him and buried her face against his shirt. He was more than a foot taller than she was, and as she stood on the very tips of her toes to reach him, it almost seemed as if he was sweeping her off her feet.

She ended the embrace and regained her footing, refusing to let him see the ache that being near him caused.

"Come in," she told him.

He thanked her and crossed the threshold, his boots sounding on the hardwood floor. He had a rugged way about him, the kind of cowboy confidence that appealed to her. Having him around wasn't going to be easy.

"Something in here smells good," he said.

"It's beef stew. Would you like some?"

"Yeah, sure. That sounds great."

Well, there you go, she thought. He'd reacted quickly once again, accepting a meal without hesitation. She didn't doubt he was going to want their conversation to happen fast, too.

She offered him a seat at the kitchen table. Her house was neat and cozy, with simple furnishings she'd purchased at flea markets and yard sales. Her favorite items to decorate with were crocheted doilies and antique mason jars. She routinely filled the jars with wildflowers, picking them herself nearly every day, since they grew freely on her property.

"I've got some coleslaw in the fridge," she said as she removed flatware from the drawer. "Would you like some of that, as well?"

He watched her move about the kitchen. "I'll take whatever you've got."

"Then, I'll warm up some bread, too." She tried to keep from getting self-conscious. He was looking at her as if he was remembering how it felt to kiss her and touch her and put his naked body next to hers. "I baked it yesterday."

He continued to watch her, much too closely. "You bake your own bread? That's cool."

"I bake pies, cakes and cookies, too."

His smile returned, only it was slightly crooked this time, giving him a strangely boyish edge, especially for a man so big and broad. "I think I'm going to enjoy hanging out with you again, Bridget."

He wasn't here to hang out with her. He was here to meet their son. But she didn't correct him, because they both knew darn well why he'd come back to Flower River.

She prepared their plates and put a basket of the warmed bread on the table, along with a stick of butter.

As she poured two glasses of water, she fought to keep her hands steady. He was still keeping a dark and masculine eye on her. Finally, she sat down across from him, trying to look more composed than she felt.

He reached for his fork. "I can't remember the last time I had a home-cooked meal. Not that you made this specifically for me. But it's still nice."

"I did make it with you in mind." She wasn't going to pretend otherwise. "I took a few days off from work, too, so I'd be around when you and Cody are getting acquainted."

"Do you still work at your family's farm equipment store?"

"Yes. And we sell more than farm equipment now. We carry feed and pet supplies, too."

"Well, I'm glad you took a few days off. It'll be easier having you around when I'm talking to Cody. I'm uncertain about what to say to him."

"That shouldn't be a problem. He's a chatterbox, so I'm sure he'll get the conversation going. He'll probably ask you tons of questions. He wants to know everything about you."

Kade buttered a slice of bread and dipped it into the stew. "I want to know all about him, too. But I haven't decided how long I'm going to stay. I'm just going to play it by ear. For now, I checked into the motel where I stayed last time. That old place is still there."

The place where they'd spent that glorious week together. She reached for her water. "It's the only motel in town."

"I know. But it doesn't look as if it's changed a bit.

You have, though. Not so much in the way you look, but the way you carry yourself. Motherhood suits you."

She felt her lonely heart go *bump.* "I love being a mom." Being a single parent, however, wouldn't have been her first choice. It wasn't what she'd envisioned for herself.

"I'm sorry that I never called you, Bridget. If I'd known how important it was, I would have."

"I took you at your word. But I should have known better."

A frown furrowed his brow. "You still should have called me when you found out you were expecting. I had the right to know that you were having my baby."

She took a jittery breath, preparing to relay the explanation he was waiting to hear. "I really liked you, Kade. I was smitten from the moment I met you. But I hadn't intended to sleep with you. I'd never done anything like that before."

"Had a fling?"

"Had sex at all. You were my first."

He flinched, good and hard. "Damn, Bridget. You're full of surprises. It never even occurred to me. I had no idea."

"It's not always that obvious."

"Why didn't you say anything?"

"I didn't want to put that kind of pressure on either of us beforehand. And after it was over, I didn't need to explain since there was no real evidence of it."

He scrunched up his face. "I hope I didn't hurt you."

"It was a little uncomfortable at first. But after that…" She let her words drift, recalling how wild and sexy and dreamy it had been.

"So I wasn't too rough or anything?"

"No. You didn't do anything wrong. I just didn't want to point out that I was a twenty-year-old virgin."

"Even if that's what you were?"

"I'd done other things. I'd just never gone all the way with anyone."

"Then, why did you do it with me?"

"Because being with you was exciting. You weren't like any of the boys I'd dated around here. Plus, when you told me that you didn't pick up women like that, it made me feel special."

"You were special. I have fond memories of you, more than anyone else I've ever been with."

"That's nice to know, but it doesn't change anything. You still drifted off the way my dad did. He was always on the road, too. A tractor salesman who blew into town and started romancing my mom. He didn't disappear right away, though. He used to come and go, even after I was born."

"So he knew about you from the start?"

"Yes. My mother told him, but he didn't offer to marry her or get too domestic. He just breezed in and out of our lives, charming us with his tales of being on the road. He used to bring me gifts from all of the places he'd been, little trinkets from his sales routes."

"Where did he live?"

"Nowhere in particular. He had a travel trailer that he hauled around. He used to say that having a home on wheels was the best way to live."

Kade squinted, as if he was listening intently to her story. "So what happened? Did he just stop coming around?"

Bridget nodded. "I was seven the last time I saw him, and I remember clinging to him and not wanting to let go. By then, his visits were becoming less frequent and he was hardly bringing any gifts anymore, so I was already starting to feel a sense of neglect. His disinterest in my mom was showing, too. It was foolish of her to wait around for him all those years, hoping that he'd want to marry her someday and turn us into a real family."

Kade squinted again. "That was a terrible thing for him to do, to disappear like that."

"He didn't disappear completely. He called one final time from the road and told my mom that he wasn't coming back. That it was too much pressure, and he couldn't handle it."

"Is that what you thought I would do to Cody? Is that why you didn't tell me about him?"

"I would have told you if you'd called me. But when you broke your promise and never got back in touch with me, I figured it was better to just keep you out of my child's life. To me, you were already showing signs of being like my dad. He never made good on his word, either. Even when he was active in our lives, we could never quite count on him. If he said he was coming for Christmas, he would show up on New Year's instead."

"I understand why your experiences with your dad triggered concerns about me. But you never even gave me a chance when you found out about the baby. I still don't think that was fair."

"Maybe not. But you have your chance now. Only whatever you do, please don't make promises to Cody that you don't intend to keep. I couldn't bear for him go through what I went through."

"I have no idea what type of relationship Cody and

I are going to establish, but I'm not your dad, Bridget. I'm not going to leave without ever coming back."

"I hope not," she said, praying with all her might that Kade turned out to be a far better man than she'd given him credit for.

Chapter Two

Kade wanted to prove himself. He wanted to do everything right. But the pressure Bridget was putting on him wasn't helping. He could tell from her expression that she had doubts.

"Were you scared when you first found out you were pregnant?" he asked.

"Are you kidding? I was terrified."

"I'm terrified, too. Except that I'm becoming a parent to a fifth-grader, instead of a newborn."

Kade was immersed in all sorts of emotions. Not only would he be meeting his son for the first time, he also had to contend with the fact that he'd been Bridget's first lover. He'd never been anyone's first. If he'd known, he might've ended it before it had begun. Then again, maybe he would've forged ahead anyway. Either way, it altered the experience when the details were clearly different from the way he'd been remembering them.

He said, "I'm trying to make up for lost time, Bridget. But I would've been here all along if I'd known that Cody existed."

"Been here how?" Her blue eyes locked onto his. "Would you have moved to Montana or offered to marry me? Somehow, I don't see it as having gone in that direction."

"You're right. I wouldn't have done either of those things. But I would have come around to see my son. I would have been his dad, regardless of my loner lifestyle."

"Like my dad did with me?" she asked, and then winced. "I'm sorry. I didn't mean to bring him up again."

Troubled by her response, he studied her. Scattered beams of sunlight slipped in from the window, enhancing the blondness of her hair and the fairness of her skin, making her look far too touchable.

Instead of caving in to the silence bouncing between them, he played devil's advocate, asking her a hypothetical question. "Just for argument's sake, if I would've offered to marry you, would you have even accepted my proposal?"

She frowned. "What kind of question is that, especially when you said it wouldn't have happened?"

"I just want to know how you would have reacted if I'd done it."

"Truthfully?" She answered him head-on. "I probably would have accepted."

He shifted in his seat, realizing the blunder he'd made. He'd expected her to say that she wouldn't have become his wife, not in any shape or form. "What about your distrustful opinion of me? How would that have factored into it?"

"If you'd offered to marry me, that would have made you seem more trustworthy."

He tried another tactic. "Even though you barely knew me?"

"Yes, but it doesn't matter." She glanced away. "It wouldn't have worked anyway. Besides, our focus is supposed to be on you getting to know Cody, not on how idealistic I would have been to marry someone who was practically a stranger."

"Lots of people get married because of babies." It was the reason his parents had ended up in their disastrous situation, with Kade being the kid they'd conceived. Of course, they'd gone on to have more children before they'd gotten divorced. "It happens all the time, even if it shouldn't."

"I know, but what's the point of talking about it? It's water under the bridge now."

"I shouldn't have brought it up. I have the tendency to speak my mind, even when I should keep quiet. I used to get in trouble for it when I was young. I spent half of my adolescent life in detention. But I acted out purposely because I didn't want to go home after school, especially when my dad was around."

"Was your father mean?"

"Yeah. He was demanding as hell, and a lot of his anger was directed at me. I used to stand up to him, and that made him even madder. But I don't have anything to do with him anymore. None of us kids do now that we're older."

"I didn't even know there were other kids. You didn't

mention them last time you and I were together. Other than saying that you were originally from LA and that you get your Native American blood from your mom's side, you didn't tell me about your family."

"I have a younger brother and sister." He would've preferred to leave his sister out of it, but he couldn't evade the truth. "Tanner is thirty-three, and Meagan is twenty-five. Both of them are still in California. But it's not all sunshine and roses out there, not for my sister anyway. She got into some trouble with the law and is serving time."

Bridget's eyes grew wide. "She's in prison?"

He nodded. "She embezzled from the place where she worked. It's just so hard for me grasp. She was such a sweet and spunky kid, and now she's a criminal." He heaved a thick sigh. "I had another baby sister, too, who came along about eight years after Meagan. But she died of SIDS."

"Oh, Kade, I'm sorry."

"Our mom is also gone now. She had a heart attack a couple of years ago. Thankfully it was before Meagan got arrested. That would have destroyed Mom."

"Grandpa is the only person close to me who ever died, and his passing still hurts."

"Losing someone you love is painful." He still mourned his mom. He still said prayers for his infant sister, too. "You never really get over it."

"You're right," she said somberly, and they finished eating. When they were done, he helped her clear the table. While she was rinsing the dishes, he stood off to the side, wishing their conversation hadn't been so serious.

Finally she cut into the quiet and said, "I'd show you

Cody's room, but he wants to bring you in there himself. He worked really hard to clean it up. Normally it's a mess."

"Then, I certainly won't sneak a peek." He wouldn't spoil it for the boy.

"I can take you outside if you'd like." She dried her hands on a plain white towel. "Cody won't mind if I give you a tour of the barn and the yard."

"Are you sure?"

"I already checked with him." She laughed a little. "We had a big discussion about what I was permitted to do."

Kade laughed, too, amused by their son's rules. "That's quite a bossy kid we've got."

"That's for sure." She turned to look at him and suddenly their gazes locked, their humor quickly fading.

He held his breath, feeling as if he was getting sucked into a vacuum. He wasn't sure how he was going to sleep at the motel tonight and not think about her. If he could kiss her, he would, just for the much-needed pleasure it would provide. But he couldn't let something like that happen, so he followed her outside, fighting the feeling.

Bridget led Kade through the back door, wondering how they could talk and laugh one minute, then stare longingly at each other the next. It was like being in one of those carnival fun houses, where you couldn't find your way out of the mazes and mirrors. Between his penchant for speaking his mind and her desperate admission that she might've actually agreed to marry him, the past was coming back to haunt her in ways she'd never imagined.

But she didn't want to think about that, not while they were standing in her yard, surrounded by her favorite wildflowers.

Determined to stay centered, to draw strength from the environment, she said, "When I was a kid, this neighborhood was part of a planned community, so most of the houses were built on one- and two-acre lots, rather than being too spread out. They never did get around to paving all the roads, though. Or maybe they never really meant to." She pointed to the side of her property. "That road leads to where my mom and grandma live. They're on the same street, just a few houses apart."

"It's convenient that you live so close to them."

"When Mom and I are at work, Grandma keeps an eye on Cody. But it's different now that Grandpa is gone. He and Cody spent a lot of time at the river. I love it there, too. It's the area this town is known for, where the farms and ranches and recreational spots are."

Kade shifted his stance. Behind him, the sky stretched like a big blue canvas. "That's why I came here all those years ago and gave that clinic. I wanted to establish a presence with the horse breeders out that way. I never really did, though."

"I'll bet you'd impress the heck out of them now."

"Yeah, I probably would. I might've back then, too, if I'd returned to do more clinics, letting them get to know me a little better."

She searched his gaze. "Then, why didn't you?"

"I don't know. Maybe it was because you were here and it might've started something that I wouldn't have known how to finish. Maybe in some unconscious way, avoiding you was deliberate on my part."

"And now you're back with the prospect of being a father to the son I deliberately didn't tell you about."

He reached out as if he meant to tame a strand of her hair that was blowing across her face, but he lowered his hand without making the connection. "We're quite a pair, you and me."

A mixed-up pair, she thought, wishing he would have touched her yet glad that he hadn't. She batted the errant hair away herself. Before things got too awkward, she asked, "Does your family know about Cody?"

"Yes, and my brother is excited that he has a ten-year-old nephew. Shocked, but excited. I think you'd like Tanner. Cody probably would, too. Tanner just settled down with his fiancée and a baby girl he's helping raise."

"Whose baby? His fiancée's?"

"No. It's Meagan's kid."

She started. "Your sister has a baby?"

He nodded. "Meagan discovered that she was pregnant soon after she was incarcerated. Her old boyfriend, the baby's father, is part of the reason she stole the money to begin with, and now he wants nothing to do with her or their child. So she asked Tanner to be her daughter's legal guardian."

"It's admirable that your brother took responsibility. But it's sad that your sister is locked up like that." And the fact that her boyfriend abandoned her and the baby was equally disturbing. "When will she be released?"

"In about two years. I haven't seen her since she's been in prison. I haven't met my niece yet, either. But I plan to. The baby is about five months old now. Tanner sends me pictures to keep me up to date, and he says she's growing like a weed. Her name is Ivy, so it seems fitting."

"That's cute." Bridget thought about how quickly Cody had grown. "Are you angry at Meagan? Is that why you haven't visited her?"

"I'm not angry, just disappointed. Meagan and I were close when she was little, but as time went on, we drifted apart. I think it's because I've been gone for so much of her life. With the age difference between us, she was just a kid when I went off to college. And after that, I started traveling the way I do."

To Bridget, that was just more proof of how his life-style might affect Cody in the same way. But she didn't call him out on it. Instead, she questioned him about his sister. "Are you ever going to try to get close to Meagan again?"

"I don't know. Now that she's in prison, I'm not sure how to do that. It's weird how both of us are on the fringes of our children's lives. I never thought I'd have that in common with her."

As they passed the arena and headed to the barn, she thought about her own family ties. "My grandmother thinks I should have told you about Cody from the beginning."

"Really?" Kade reacted with immediate interest. "And what about your mom? How does she feel about all of this?"

"She's concerned about your character and whether you'll be worthy of Cody. But after what she went through with my dad, she's bound to be cautious."

Kade turned pensive, stopping just short of the barn. "During the years he was around, did he provide any kind of support?"

"You mean financially? No. Mom never asked for anything from him. She just clung to the quiet dream of marrying him someday."

"I want to help with Cody. I want to arrange for child support."

"That isn't necessary." She didn't want this to be about money. "I can give my son what he needs. I've been taking care of him since he was born." And she wasn't keen on changing the rules.

"If you won't accept support from me, then I'll set up a trust for him. At least that way, I can put something aside for his future."

"If that's the way you want to handle it, that's fine. I appreciate that you want to provide a nest egg for him. But I don't want you making payments to me." She wished he wasn't towering over her with that big broad body of his, intensifying her awareness of him. "I'm more comfortable keeping things as they've been."

"I'm just trying to do what a dad is supposed to do. Besides, I have a sound portfolio. I've been making investments for years." He made a grand gesture. "I could buy myself a big ole ranch." He lowered his hands to his sides. "But being boxed in would probably make me panic."

"Most people wouldn't think of owning a large spread as being boxed in."

"It's not the size of the place. It's the act of putting down roots. Even when I was a kid, I felt stifled every time I walked into the house, and I promised myself that I when I grew up, I would go wherever the wind took me."

And now the wind was blowing him in this direction. But for how long, she couldn't be sure. She wanted to trust him, to believe that he would be as responsible with Cody as he claimed he would be, but it was too soon to take him at his word.

"We need to lighten things up," he said.

Bridget blinked. "What?"

"All of this heavy conversation. We didn't do that last time."

Did he expect it to be the same? "The circumstances were different."

"I know, but what's wrong with being upbeat, like we were before?" He flashed a cheesy smile, showing way too many teeth.

She went ahead and laughed. "You look like Dudley Do-Right."

He laughed, too. "The dimwitted Mountie with the horse named Horse? I saw that movie. I think it got just about the worst reviews ever."

"I know, but I thought Dudley was cute."

He upped his hundred-watt smile. "So you had a thing for him?"

"I was a teenager when I had that crush." She batted her lashes, being as silly as he was. "But a girl likes what she likes, I guess."

"Big dumb guys with rockin' bodies?" he teased her, flexing like a brainless stud.

His Dudley Do-Right smile was pretty near blinding her now. And damn if he didn't live up to the rockin'-body part. She almost grabbed his arm by the biceps, but thought better of it. Instead, she simply said, "Come on. Let's go see the horses."

They entered the barn, and the equines came forward and poked their heads over the stalls, interested, no doubt, as to who Kade was.

"Well, hello you two," he said, approaching them like newfound friends. "I take it neither of you is named Horse?"

"Sorry, no." Bridget introduced the gray. "That's Misty. She's a gentle old girl, but when the mood strikes, she can get barn sour." She turned to the red dun. "And that's Minnie P. She's a bit of a nut so we named her after Minnie Pearl, the country comedienne who used to wear the sales tag on her hat. My grandfather loved the Grand Ole Opry, and he thought Minnie Pearl was the best."

Kade chuckled and gave the horse an affectionate pat. "That's quite a handle to live up to. Almost as bad as Horse." He shifted his attention to Misty, patting her, too. "As for this old gal, I can help you with her. I've got plenty of remedies for barn sour horses."

"That would be great. We've only had her for about six months, so she's still fairly new to us. I got her at an auction, and I'm the one who rides her. She'll be fine for a while, then she starts getting stubborn again."

"No problem. Maybe we can have a training session later this week?"

"Okay. That sounds good." Just for the heck of it, she showed him the rest of the barn, even if there wasn't much to see, other than the tack room and hayloft.

After the tour, they went back outside, and he removed his phone from his pocket and checked the time. "It's almost two," he said. "What time does Cody get home?"

"Around three. We can meet him at the bus stop."

"What should we do between now and then?"

She considered his question. The next hour was going to seem like forever if she didn't think of something to keep them occupied. "I can make a pot of coffee if you need a boost."

"Sounds good. I can always use a shot of caffeine."

"Do you still take it with tons of sugar?"

He looked surprised. "You remember how I take my coffee? That's a hell of memory you've got there."

She wasn't likely to forget. "I take mine supersweet, too, and every time we went to the diner next to the motel, we had to ask for more of those little packets. There was never enough on the table."

His lips curved into an instant smile. "Ah, yes, my sugar partner in crime. Now that you mention it, it's coming back to me, too. It's funny because when I checked into the motel, I noticed that the diner is still there, and from what I saw, it looks pretty much the same."

"Cheap motels and greasy spoons never die."

He put away his phone. "And neither do sexy memories."

"There's nothing sexy about that diner."

"I was talking about the motel."

Before she got weak-kneed and shivery, she started walking toward the house. No way was she going to add fuel to the fire by saying anything else.

Once they were in the kitchen, she stood at the counter, preparing to make the coffee. He leaned over her shoulder, watching the process. She wanted to tell him to give her some space, but she liked his nearness, too.

For now, her mind was filled with images of the motel and how they'd conceived Cody. They'd used protection, except for when they were in the shower. It hadn't been very responsible of them, but they'd both been of the same mindset, wanting to feel that kind of physical closeness without a barrier between them.

Were those the sexy memories he was referring to? She remembered it well: the water pouring down over them, their mouths fused in blind need, her pulling him closer, him withdrawing at the moment of completion in an attempt to minimize the risk.

"What are you thinking about, Bridget?"

She nearly spilled the roasted grounds she was scooping into the machine but forced herself to finish making the coffee. "I was just zoning out."

He was still leaning over her shoulder. "I've been doing that, too, getting caught up in all kinds of thoughts. Mostly I've been thinking about Cody, hoping he likes me as much as he thinks he will."

Warmed by his admission, Bridget turned to look at him, and they gazed gently at each other.

She broke eye contact and poured the coffee, which was already filling the room with a homey aroma.

She handed him the sugar bowl, but he gave it back to her, letting her go first. She didn't know how something as mundane as adding sweetener to her drink could elevate her already heightened emotions. But God help her, it did.

He took his turn and they remained quiet, sipping the sugar-laden brew and waiting for the moment to arrive for him to meet their son.

Chapter Three

Cody's bus stop was located on the corner of a paved street, just blocks from Bridget's house. Kade struggled to stand still, but it wasn't the coffee he'd drunk that was affecting him. It was his nerves.

"Are more parents going to be showing up?" he asked Bridget. For now, they were the only people there, but they were also about ten minutes early.

"I'm pretty sure we'll be it," she replied. "The kids who get off at this stop are old enough to walk home by themselves."

"Then, maybe we shouldn't be doing this. Maybe Cody will feel stupid about us being here."

"Are you kidding? He's going to feel like a million bucks when he sees you. It will be the surprise of his young life."

"Yeah, but he already knows I was coming today. Maybe he would prefer to meet me at the house."

"Don't worry about it. He's going to be ecstatic to see you standing here. So just try to relax, okay?"

Easier said than done. Kade was as anxious as an expectant father in a maternity ward. Bridget, however, didn't have the look of woman who was about to give birth, not with those sexy curves of hers or all that soft blond hair shining in the sun.

Curious about the day his son had come wailing into the world, he asked, "Who was with you when Cody was born?"

She smoothed the front of her blouse, and then placed a hand against her stomach in what seemed like a gesture of remembrance. "My whole family was there. Mom, Grandma, Grandpa."

"Did any of them go into the delivery room with you?"

"My mom did. She stayed by my side the entire time, coaching me to breathe and push and all of that."

Kade had gone to the hospital after his youngest sister was born and peered at her tiny face through the glass, but he hadn't been directly involved in the birthing process. He'd helped plenty of mares during foaling, though, and loved the beauty of new life. "Was your labor difficult?"

"It wasn't easy, but it wasn't especially difficult, either. Mostly it just seemed surreal. Me having a baby at the same hospital where I was born. An unwed mother just as my mom had been. In her day, that carried a bit of stigma. But her friends didn't treat her badly because of it. They wanted my dad to settle down and offer to marry her." Bridget continued to hold her hand against her stomach. "But after he quit coming around, they just felt sorry for us."

He couldn't help from asking, "How much do your friends know about me?"

"My close friends know the truth. But I've never confided in any casual acquaintances. Of course, the way Cody has been bragging about you lately, I'm sure that people are getting curious."

"Yeah, and once they see me, their tongues are really going to start wagging. A tall drink of water like me is hard to miss."

She shot him an amused look. "Did you just refer to yourself as a tall drink of water?"

He shrugged, but he smiled, too. He liked making this kind of banter with her. "That's what women call me."

"Really?" Her blue eyes all but sparkled. "What women?"

"The kind who check me out." He motioned to the house behind them. "I'll bet there's a hottie at that window right now, eyeing my butt."

"I know the hottie who lives there and she's about eighty years old and plays bingo with my grandmother."

He laughed and bumped her shoulder. "I play a mean bingo myself."

She nudged him right back. "Don't tell Grandma that. She'll be dragging you to the senior center with her."

He contemplated what she'd told him earlier, about her grandmother thinking he should have been notified about Cody from the start. "At least Granny is on my side."

"She's definitely going to like you."

"I appreciate that." He needed an ally. "By the way, I have a gift for Cody in my truck. I didn't want to show up empty-handed." He quickly clarified, "And this doesn't make me like your dad, Bridget. I don't think giving gifts means that I can neglect my responsibilities as a father. It's just something I want Cody to have."

"Okay. I understand. But what is it?"

He decided to keep the details of the gift a mystery. "You'll just have to wait and see." As far as he was concerned, he was invoking some of the rights he'd lost and taking his first step toward being a parent. "I shouldn't have to get your approval every time I give him something."

"Yes, you should. We should discuss everything that concerns our son."

"We are discussing it."

She rolled her eyes, but she let it pass, giving him a taste of freedom. While he was basking in his victory, she redirected his attention.

"Look," she said. "There's Cody's bus."

Kade spun around and saw the yellow vehicle rolling down the street, and within the beat of his heart, his big, bad confidence flew by the wayside. The man he'd always been, the loner who panicked at the sight of commitment, was as scared as a rabbit on the run. Only he wasn't running. He was standing there, boots firmly planted, where the bus was preparing to stop.

The first to disembark was a girl, a brunette he guessed to be about Cody's age. She crossed the street and headed off by herself. The next two kids were also girls, redheads who appeared to be twins. He almost did a double take when he saw them. He figured them for around twelve. They acknowledged Bridget as they passed and gave Kade nosy glances.

Cody appeared at the top of the bus steps, looking

exactly like his pictures. His cowlick was misbehaving, causing pieces of his hair to spring in different directions, and as soon as he saw Kade, his mouth fell open.

Another boy, a freckled redhead who resembled the girls who'd just gone by, was behind him saying, "Oh, man. Is that your dad?" and giving him an excited little shove. The driver, a middle-aged woman, reprimanded the ginger-haired boy, who Kade figured was probably the younger brother of the nosy twins.

It was like watching a movie and being part of it at the same time. Cody finally exited the vehicle and walked up to Kade. For a kid who was supposed to be chatty, he was being awfully quiet.

The other boy gawked at them as he made his way down the steps, nearly tripping on the road as his feet hit the ground.

"That's my friend," Cody said. "His name is Jason."

"Hi, Jason." Kade gave him a quick wave. He'd never expected Cody's first words to him to be about someone else.

"Hi," Jason replied with a toothy grin. As he walked off, his smile still in place, he said, "See ya, Cody."

"Bye." Cody grinned, too.

And what a smile. Kade could hardly breathe. Should he shake his son's hand? Lean down to hug him? Smooth his hair?

"You surprised me," Cody said, staring at him in what could only be described as wonder. By now, more kids were getting off the bus and looking their way.

Kade couldn't take credit for the surprise. "It was your mom's idea."

Cody glanced over at her. "My dad's really here, and at my bus stop, too, where everyone can see him."

"Yes, he's really here." Bridget came forward. "Why don't we all go back to the house and I'll make you guys a snack."

"Are you hungry?" Cody asked Kade.

Food was the furthest thing from his mind. He was still having trouble breathing. But he didn't want to put a damper on the mood so he said, "Your mom already fed me earlier, but I can always eat."

"Me, too." Cody shifted his backpack. "What's your favorite food?"

And that was how the Q&A session began. The ten-year-old interviewed him on the walk home, relentless in his pursuit to know his father. Kade could barely keep up with the rapid succession of questions, so he merely spouted whatever came to mind off the top of his head.

"Jeez, kiddo," his mom said as they entered the front door. "Give the man a chance to think."

"Am I bugging you?" Cody asked, gazing up at him with soulful eyes.

"No, not at all." He finally took a chance and touched his son's hair, smoothing the strands in front, which didn't do a bit of good. They popped right back up. "You could never bug me."

"See, Mom?" the youngster said. "He likes me asking him questions."

Kade looked over at Bridget, feeling beautifully overwhelmed by the child they'd made. Cody Colton Wells was sweet and funny and spirited. She returned his gaze, and they stared at each other over the top of their son's head.

"I'm going to show Dad my room," Cody said to her.

Kade's heart punched his chest. He'd just officially been called Dad.

"Go ahead." If Bridget noticed, she didn't let on. But she did give both father and son a wobbly smile. "I'll cut up some apples and cheese and bring it to you."

By now, Kade's appetite was coming back, so the food was starting to sound good. Or maybe it was just the idea of sharing a snack with his kid. Either way, he was up for it.

"Bring us some cookies, too," Cody said as he tugged Kade down the hall.

"You know better than that," his mother called back. "You can't come home and load up on sweets."

Cody huffed out a breath. "She's the one who bakes all that stuff, then she gets mad at me if I eat too much of it. She's kind of strict about other things, too. Maybe you can loosen her up."

Kade almost laughed. Cody certainly had a way about him. "I don't know about that, but I wouldn't mind a few cookies."

"Dad wants some cookies!" the kid shouted loud enough to rock the house. Then he lowered his voice and gave Kade a lopsided grin. "She can't refuse now 'cause you're a guest."

At that mischief-making moment, Cody reminded him of Meagan when she was the same age. Kade's sister had been full of spit and vinegar, too. Of course, that wasn't a good comparison, not now that Meagan was a convict.

Cody's room consisted of a platform-style bed draped with a brown quilt, a rugged dresser, a student desk, lots of cluttered shelves and a bank of windows with a view of the backyard.

"This is probably the cleanest it's ever been," Cody said, repeating what Bridget had mentioned earlier.

"Usually I just leave my dirty clothes on the floor instead of putting them in the hamper. Sometimes I leave other stuff on the floor, too, and it drives Mom crazy when she trips over things. You should hear her go off. Grandpa used to say that Mom can curse like a sailor when she thinks no one is listening." He plopped down on the bed. "But I put everything away since you were coming."

Kade couldn't have been more amused. "I appreciate you cleaning up for me. Now your mom doesn't have to break her neck."

"Or curse like a sailor," Cody reminded him.

"That, too." Kade sat in the chair at the desk, turning it around to face the bed.

Cody leaned forward and asked, "Do you like to draw?"

"Actually, I do." Of all the questions so far, it was one of the easiest to answer. "I majored in equine science in college. But I also took some art classes, just for my own enjoyment."

"Wow. That's so cool. I love to draw. Mostly comic book–type stuff. I even make my own comic books. What kind of art do you do?"

"I like to sketch landscapes and wildlife and things like that. Horses, too, of course." Kade quickly asked, "Do you think I could see some of your work?"

"Sure." Cody bobbed up and riffled through the shelves, producing a stack of comic books he'd made.

As Kade paged through them, he was more than impressed. Cody was a fine little artist. The superheroes he created were down-home guys, fishermen and horsemen who got their powers from taking secret trips to

Mars. There was even a farmer who glowed in the dark and flew around on a bullet-shaped tractor.

"These are excellent," Kade said.

"Thanks." The kid beamed. "I won an art contest at my school last year."

"I'm not surprised. You could make a living at this someday." Kade noticed that one of the comic books featured superhero Natives who lived on a space-aged reservation. "Did you know that I'm part Cheyenne?"

"Yep. Mom told me. She always wanted me to know who I was and where I came from. She was just worried that you traveled too much and wouldn't be around like a dad should be."

Kade supposed that this was a conversation that needed to happen, especially since Cody was a no-holds-barred type of kid. "I like being on the road and traveling for my work, but it's not going to stop me from being your father. You're my priority now that I know about you."

"Mom's dad just went away one day and never came back."

"I know. She told me about him. But I'm never going to do that to you."

"You better not, or Mom will kill you."

Cody's warning sounded quite serious. But Kade already knew it was no joking matter. "I won't do anything to hurt either of you."

"I trust you." The boy drew his knees up. "But Mom isn't going to be so easy on you. I heard girls are like that, though."

"They can be. Or so I've heard, as well." Kade wasn't an authority on the opposite sex. "Is there a girl you like at school?"

"No." Cody said it with disgust or embarrassment or whatever it was that was going on in his young mind. Then he asked, "Do you still like my mom?"

Now, that was a loaded question if there ever was one, but he did his best to supply a ready answer. "I still think she's sweet and pretty. And I'm hoping that she and I will become friends again."

"It's taking her a long time to get our snack. But she's probably being slow on purpose to give us time to talk."

"Yeah, I'm sure that's it." And talking they were. Important subjects were being bandied about. "I brought a gift for you. It's out in my truck, but I'd rather give it to you while your mom is here, so we'll wait for her."

"Really? You got something for me? I can hurry Mom up. I can tell her to get cracking."

"No, that's okay. Let's just—"

Too late. Cody was already at the doorway yelling, "Mom! Hurry up! Dad has a present for me!"

Kade had a lot to learn, apparently. Such as not mentioning a gift before you planned on giving it.

Bridget appeared soon enough, carrying a tray with diced apples, cheddar cheese, chocolate-chip cookies and two frosty glasses of milk. "So you told him that you brought him something?"

"Yep. And he doesn't want to wait."

She placed the tray on the dresser. "You should see him on Christmas morning."

"I can only imagine."

"Come on, you guys," Cody said. "Let's get this done. Otherwise I'll be too anxious to eat the snack."

Kade looked to Bridget for guidance, and she nodded her acquiescence. Cody had won both the cookie and the get-me-my-present battle, even with his supposedly strict mother.

"I'll go out to my truck now," Kade said. As he left the room, he felt Bridget and their son watching him, knowing darn well they were going to talk about him after he was gone.

Bridget sat next to Cody on the bed, and he sent her an excited smile.

"Dad is so awesome, Mom. He likes to draw and everything. He even took art classes in college. He thinks I could make a living with my comic books someday. Oh, and he promised he'd never go away and not come back. You were wrong about him. He's not the same as your dad."

"I'm glad you like him." But she'd expected as much. Cody already had been building a preconceived notion of his father as a hero, and all Bridget could do was keep hoping and praying that Kade didn't let him down.

"Did he tell you what my present is?"

"No, he didn't."

"Do you think he'll bring me something every time he visits?"

"I have no idea. But this isn't about getting gifts."

"I know. I was just asking what you thought. I asked him if he still likes you, and he said he still thinks you're sweet and pretty. He wants to be friends with you again."

She wished Cody hadn't brought her into it. She was already feeling the heat of being near Kade, of being far too attracted to him. Thinking of him as a friend wasn't on her radar, but she knew it should be that way, especially for Cody's sake.

Kade returned with a medium-size box. He hadn't wrapped it, though, not like Bridget's dad used to do with her gifts.

He placed it on the bed next to Cody. "Here you go."

Their son clutched it with glee. "Can I shake it first?"

"Sure. Go ahead." Kade smiled as he stood beside the dresser, looking tall and dark and cowboy delicious.

Bridget warned herself not to gaze at him with stars in her eyes. She wasn't a twenty-year-old girl anymore. She'd grown up since then.

Cody shook the heck out of the box, but nothing rattled. He got up and went to his desk and grabbed a pair of scissors.

"Be careful," Bridget said as he attacked the tape on the box.

"I know, Mom, I know." He glanced at Kade as if to say *women*, making her wonder if the temperament of females had been part of their father/son discussion.

Cody got the box open and tore away the packing material. The gift itself was another box, only it was made of aluminum.

"It's a time capsule," Kade said. "You're supposed to put things in that are important to you. Artifacts from your life that you'd want historians to uncover years and years from now. Then you bury it someplace safe. You can even register it online with the company I bought it from so you never forget where you buried it."

"Oh, wow. Thank you so much." Cody was over the moon. "Check this out, Mom. A time capsule."

Bridget figured that Cody would be excited regardless of what it was, simply because it had come from his dad. But she was impressed by what an unusual gift it was. "That was a very clever idea, Kade."

He replied, "I made one myself when I was about Cody's age. It was just a coffee can with a plastic lid, so there was no way it was going to stand the test of time. But I didn't know that then."

Cody was all ears, listening to his dad's tale, and so was Bridget, caught in the fascination of it all.

He continued the story. "I got my brother, Tanner, involved. He would have been about seven at the time. I told him to gather up some things so we could put everything in the time capsule together."

"What type of stuff did you choose?" Cody asked.

"Tanner had a truck-and-trailer toy set that he favored, but he wasn't willing to part with it. Instead, he contributed one of the little plastic horses that came with it. He tossed in a tiny snap-on saddle, too. I put in a drawing of a palomino I'd done. It was the horse our mom was leasing for us to ride, and its name was Brandy. I signed and dated the picture to make it official. I also put in one of my report cards to provide more information about who I was. I grabbed one of Tanner's report cards, too, to identify him."

Cody opened the top of his time capsule and peered inside. Then he glanced up and asked, "Where'd you bury it after you were done filling it?"

"We went to the rental stables where Brandy was being boarded. It was within walking distance from our house. We brought a backpack filled with gardening tools and then found a spot where no one was around and buried it."

"What do you think happened to it?"

"It probably got destroyed by groundwater. But it was a great memory, and I thought you might enjoy doing something like that, too, except with a time capsule that will last. This one won't get corroded. It's a professional model."

"I totally want to do it." Cody was bouncing on his heels. "Do you want to do it with me? We could both put stuff in here. It's plenty big enough."

"Sure," Kade told him. "I'd love to participate. I already bought you a preservation kit to go with it. That's still out in my truck. It comes with packets and pouches and envelopes so you can separate items. There's a fade-proof pencil for labeling everything, too."

Cody looked at Bridget. "How about you, Mom? Will you do it with us? It could be like a family project."

A family project. To her, that was far more complicated than it sounded, making her and Kade seem like a couple. But she couldn't refuse, not with the anticipation and excitement in her son's eyes.

"Of course I will," she said. "It'll be fun. I'd have to think about what to put in it, though."

Kade sought her gaze, and she felt a wave of attraction, which was particularly unwelcome because she was sitting on Cody's bed. But at least it wasn't her bed. She didn't want Kade anywhere near her bedroom.

"I'm going to make a comic book to put in it," Cody said. "A brand-new one. And it's going to be about a mom, a dad and a kid who put stuff in a time capsule, like we're going to do. But instead of historians finding it, I'm going to make it so aliens dig it up centuries later."

"That sounds like a great comic," Kade said.

Cody went silent, as if he was plotting the rest of the story. A few quick-thinking beats later, he said, "The aliens are here on earth because their planet was seized by intergalactic rebels. But what the aliens don't know at first is that the mom and dad and kid are actually superheroes who are still alive, and they're going to help the aliens save their planet."

Kade replied, "That's a perfect representation of your work, especially to go into a time capsule. I can't imagine anything better."

"I know, right? I'm going to start on it tonight."

Bridget hated to be the bearer of bad news, but she said, "Cody, don't you have homework to do tonight?"

"Yeah, but that can wait. This new comic book is way more important."

She blew out her breath. "I'm sorry, sport, but homework comes first."

"But this is a big occasion for me. Meeting my dad and preparing for our time capsule. We still have to decide where to bury to it."

Kade interjected, "Your mom's right about your homework. That should come first. We still have time to figure out the rest of it."

"How much time?" Cody asked. "How long are you going to be in town?"

"I don't know." Kade repeated what he'd told Bridget earlier. "I was just going to play it by ear." He then added, "Maybe it's something we can decide together."

Cody jumped right on it. "I get out of school in two weeks, so you should stay longer than that. Otherwise we'll hardly see each other."

"How much longer do you think I should stay?"

Cody went full bore. "How about if you hang out for the whole summer? Then we could do lots of stuff together."

The entire summer? Bridget wasn't prepared for that. She glanced at Kade, hoping he wasn't available.

Thankfully, he wasn't. He said, "I've already got plans to go to California in mid-July, so how about if I stay here until then? Of course, if I'm going to be around for that long, then I'll need to find another place to stay. Maybe I'll look into renting a fishing cabin or hunting lodge or something. I don't want to live out of a motel."

Cody took what he could get, and Bridget breathed a sigh of relief. Of course, it was still a long time for Kade to be around, but not as bad as the entire summer.

Cody asked her, "If I do my homework first, can I work on the comic afterward? 'Cause I'm going to need to get it done if Dad is only going to be here till July."

"That's fine," she told him, letting him enjoy the moment.

While she sat quietly on the sidelines, father and son continued to talk about the time capsule. They also ate the snack, both of them going after the cookies before getting to the apples and cheese.

Finally, the visit ended, with Kade saying that he needed to go back to the motel and get settled in. He hugged Cody goodbye, and the transfixed ten-year-old smiled up at him.

Cody asked Bridget if Kade could come back for dinner tomorrow, and she agreed that he could. He accepted the invitation and thanked her. Before she could save her sanity and stop him from embracing her the way he'd done when he'd first arrived, he reached out and wrapped her in the dizzying warmth of his arms all over again.

Chapter Four

The following morning Bridget's mom stopped by, but she didn't come inside. Since she was on her way to work, she preferred to stand in the graveled driveway and have a quick talk.

Still, Bridget took a moment to study her. If she wanted to see herself twenty-five years from now, all she had to do was look at the woman who'd given her life. Mom was a little heavier than she used to be, with tiny lines around her eyes and threads of gray sneaking into her natural blond hair, but the overall resemblance between them wasn't hard to miss.

"What do you think of Kade now that you've seen him again?" Mom asked, getting right to the point.

Bridget answered cautiously, not wanting to include anything too personal. "Cody certainly liked him. They clicked right away."

Her mother's face had a pinched expression. "That's what Cody told your grandmother. He called her last night before he went to bed, singing his daddy's praises. But he already idolized the man before he met him, so he's been enamored from the start. If something goes wrong, he's going to be crushed. It gives me a knot in the pit of my stomach just thinking about it."

"I know. Me, too." Bridget couldn't just wash away her fears. "But Kade keeps saying that his interest in Cody won't fade. That he'll keep coming back to visit. So I'm trying to give him the benefit of the doubt. I promised him that much."

"I suppose it's the right thing to do. But it still worries me."

"I know," Bridget said again. If anyone understood, it was her mom. "But at least they seem to have a lot in common. I didn't know that Kade took art classes in college. It never occurred to me that was where Cody might've gotten his talent. I just thought it was a random gene."

"How could you know everything about Kade? You only spent a week with him. And as much as I hate to say this, I can tell that you're still attracted to him."

So much for keeping her feelings hidden. "How can you tell? I'm just standing here."

"It's written all over your face, honey. But I suspected that it might happen. You had a strong crush on him the first time around, and now he's back, stirring your senses again."

"I'm trying to compartmentalize my feelings." And manage the temptation of being near him. "But I think it's going to take some time for me to get a handle on it."

"I wish Cody would've never taken an interest in

him." Mom swigged from the plastic water bottle she'd brought with her. "Now that your grandmother knows how pleased Cody is with Kade, she's ready to go full steam ahead. She wants to host a barbecue this Saturday, so she and I can meet Kade. But she wants to invite other people, too."

"What other people?" Everything was moving at such a breakneck pace, Bridget could hardly keep up.

"Our friends. Yours, hers, mine, Cody's. The more the merrier, according to her."

"Did she say anything to Cody about it?"

"Not yet. She wanted me to run it by you first. But she's certain that he'll be thrilled."

"She's right. He's going to love the idea of showing his dad off to everyone. I think Kade will be fine about it, too. He already knows that Grandma is on his side, so he'll probably appreciate that this was her brainstorm."

"How do you feel about introducing Kade to your friends?"

Bridget was a bit nervous about it, but she tried to keep it in perspective. "They've just start asking about him anyway, wondering what he's like and how it's going. I'll have to deal with it sooner or later. So it might as well be sooner. He's coming for dinner tonight, so I can tell him and Cody about the barbecue then."

Mom capped her water. "I hope this isn't going to seem like a twisted question, considering that I never had the courage to ask you before. But have you ever secretly wanted to search for your dad? Has it ever been a thought in your head?"

"Honestly?" Bridget made a pattern in the gravel, moving the tiny stones with the tip of her boot. "I used to fantasize about it. I'd picture myself striding up to him somewhere, and when I was close enough for him to figure out that I was the daughter he'd ditched, I would tell him in no uncertain terms how much I hated him. But even in my tough-girl fantasies, I was afraid that I might break down and cry and look like a fool. I even feared that I might discover that he was dead. Then I wouldn't be able to do anything, except feel even emptier inside."

"He could be gone by now, I suppose." Mom leaned against her truck, looking a bit empty herself. "Or he could be out there, the same as always."

Bridget turned the twisted question around. "Have you ever considered looking for him?"

"Yes, but just to learn what became of him. In the long run, though, I knew it wouldn't be worth it. With the way I loved your dad, I was afraid I would get sucked back into those feelings again."

"I always wondered about Kade, too, but I never even typed his name into the computer. That would have made it too real."

"And now here you are, with reality nipping at your heels. But I want you to know that however difficult this gets or however it unfolds, you can come to me."

"Thank you." Her heart tugged in her chest. "But I already know that I can count on you." She'd gotten shortchanged with her dad. But her mom had always been her soft place to fall.

While Bridget was immersed in making a spaghetti dinner, she glanced at Cody. He sat at the kitchen table, working on his time capsule comic and waiting for Kade to arrive. He'd already rushed through his homework, just as he'd done last night, so that he could make the comic a priority.

As soon as the doorbell rang, he dropped what he was doing and leaped up like a frog. "I'll get it!"

Bridget stayed where she was, at the stove, stirring the sauce. Within seconds, father and son entered the room.

"Hi," Kade said to her, his presence creating electric energy.

"Hi," she replied, and kept stirring. One simple exchange, one greeting, and he made her feel like an anxious virgin all over again.

"Check out what I've done so far," Cody said to his dad. "I still have lots more to do to finish it, but I'm going to keep working on it whenever I can."

Kade took a seat, openly admiring the pages that had been completed. "Oh, wow. This is amazing." He glanced up. "Have you seen it, Bridget? His drawings are of the three of us. We're the stars of his adventure."

She summoned a smile. She'd seen it, all right. Cody had turned them into a crime-fighting trio. "That's quite a costume I have on."

Cody chimed in. "I wasn't sure how to draw you, Mom. So I used other comic books with superhero girls in them as my guide, and they were all wearing these types of outfits. Only I made yours more Western."

"I think it's a wonderful likeness," Kade said to Bridget. "Like Dale Evans with a spark of Marilyn Monroe."

"Who are they?" Cody asked as Bridget narrowed her eyes at her son's dad.

"They're old-time actresses," she told him. "And really, Kade, Dale Evans?"

He chuckled. "I couldn't think of another country girl."

She made a face at him, simply to stop him from staring at her the way he was. And it could have been worse, she supposed. Cody could have drawn her to look way more momish, instead of putting her in a cat-suit with fringe and country boots.

"It kind of looks like Veronica Lake, too," Kade said to Cody. "She's another old-time actress. She had long blond hair like your mom's, only she sometimes wore it covering one of her eyes. That helped make her famous."

When Cody shrugged and went back to his work, Bridget asked Kade, "So what's the deal? Are you an old-movie buff?"

"Yeah, I guess you could say that. But I'm also an old-pinup buff. When I was a teenager, I used to go into a poster shop that had tons of classic pinups lining the walls, and I got fascinated with them. The interesting thing about Veronica Lake is most of her pinups were from the shoulders up because her hair was such a hot commodity. She was small, too, like you. I don't even think she stood five feet."

"I'm five-three." Bridget defended her stature, even though he wasn't criticizing her. If anything, he was looking at her with far too much attraction in his eyes.

He said, "When I go home to visit my family, I think I'll go see Veronica's star in Hollywood. And Marilyn's." He teased her with a wink and a smile. "I probably better check out Dale's, too, just so her feelings don't get hurt."

She shook her head, caught in his flirtation and trying not to let it show. "What about Roy and Trigger?"

"Trigger doesn't have a star. Lassie and Rin Tin Tin do, though."

Cody glanced up. "What are you guys talking about?"

Kade replied, "The Walk of Fame. The sidewalks in Hollywood that have pink-and-gold stars with famous people's names written on them. There are some famous animals' names on them, too. Even some of the Muppets have stars. Come to think of it, Godzilla has one, but as far as I know, he's the only monster so far."

"Really?" Cody's eyes lit up. He loved monster movies.

Kade added, "There are also movie-star lookalikes and people dressed up as superheroes and cartoon characters walking around. It's so the tourists can take pictures with them. For a while, though, they were banned from the streets because some of them were creating a ruckus. But I think they're back. Not all of them were causing problems."

"Oh, man. It sounds like a fun place." Cody addressed Bridget. "Doesn't it, Mom?"

To her, it sounded like a whole other crazy world. "It's certainly different from anything that goes on here."

"I grew up in Burbank," Kade told their son. "Our house was about eight miles from Hollywood. Some of the TV and movie studios are in Burbank. But it has horse facilities, too."

"Like the one where you and your brother buried your time capsule?"

"Yep, like that one. Tanner still lives in the area and has his own stables and riding academy now. He rents horses to the public, but he also leases them for movies and television."

"Dang." Cody turned to Bridget again. "Do you think we could ever go to California, Mom?"

She understood how impressed he was. Not only did his father work with prominent clients, his uncle was involved in the movie industry. But she had enough to worry about, let alone her son's sudden interest in glitz and glamour. "I don't know, sweetie. That's a long way from here."

"I can take you to California," Kade said. "I can take both of you anytime you want to go."

Bridget nearly buttered her hand instead of the garlic bread she was preparing. She took a second to breathe, calming the anxiety created by the idea of taking a trip with Kade. "I think we'd better stick to Montana."

Cody huffed out his displeasure. "We never go anywhere."

Hoping to turn his grumpy mood around, she said, "Complain all you want, but just so you know, Grandma is going to host a barbecue on Saturday so we can invite our friends to meet your dad."

That did the trick. He bobbed up and down. "Did you hear that, Dad? Did you hear what Mom just said?"

"Yes, I heard." While Cody was moving to and fro, Kade's gaze connected with Bridget's. "I'm going to be introduced to everyone at once?"

She nodded. "Sorry to spring it on you so soon, but I just found out about it this morning. Grandma wanted to do this for you and Cody."

"That's nice of her. I'm really looking forward to meeting her. She's already making me feel welcome."

Bridget doubted that her mother would do the same.

But she wasn't about to say that in front of Cody. Besides, she'd already told Kade about how leery her mom was. He wasn't expecting her to go out of her way for him. Thankfully, though, Grandma would be there to diffuse the tension, if need be.

"Is it almost time to eat?" Cody asked.

"Yes, it is," Bridget replied, grateful that he'd interrupted her thoughts. "So why don't you clear the table?"

"Okay." Cody gathered his art supplies.

As their son left the room, Kade joined Bridget at the stove, and her awareness of him kicked into high gear. No matter how hard she tried to control her attraction to him, she couldn't seem to do it.

"All of this home cooking is going to spoil me," he said.

She wished he wasn't standing so close, making her heart pound. "It's not anything fancy."

"It is to me." He moved even closer. "Can I taste the sauce? The smell of the spices has been driving me crazy."

She understood the crazy spicy feeling, and it had nothing to do with food. As she tended to the pasta boiling on the other burner, she directed him to a spoon.

He dipped it into the sauce, put it up to his mouth and made a sound of pleasure. She took a step back, moving deliberately away from him. But it didn't do any good.

Even after Cody returned and they settled in to eat, all she did was battle her appetite for Kade.

Kade walked onto the porch, where Bridget was seated in a rustic chair, gazing out at the front yard. She turned toward him, and he was struck by how alluring she looked beneath the misty veil of a sconce lantern.

"Where's Cody?" she asked.

A minute of breathless silence passed before he replied, "He crashed out on the couch. Should I carry him to bed?"

"No, that's okay. He'll wake up on his own."

"I wasn't expecting him to conk out like that." After dinner, he and Cody had played a slew of video games. Then, later, after they'd started watching a movie on TV, the kid just dozed off. "Is it my fault? Did I wear him out?"

"No." She spoke softly, almost as if she was talking to the night. "He's always like that. Don't worry about it."

"Is it all right if I sit with you?" He didn't want to go back to the motel yet. He wanted to enjoy the evening with her. "It's nice out here."

She gestured to the empty chair beside her. But what else was she going to do? Tell him to get lost? He figured she was too polite to send him on his way, even if she probably wanted to. She'd dodged him after the meal, keeping her distance. He suspected it was because of the sexy vibes that kept bouncing between them. But he thought avoiding each other would only make it worse.

He took the proffered seat. "I'll be glad when I find another place to stay. Being at the motel only makes me think of what we did there."

Her voice sounded shaky. "Please, Kade, don't say things like that."

"But it's the truth. It's a reminder of the week we spent together, and we both need to move past that."

"How is talking about it going to help?"

"It seems better than keeping it inside. Otherwise the air gets too thick around us, and we struggle to breathe."

She exhaled a noisy gust of air. "I can breathe just fine."

He laughed. "Yes, I can see how well you're doing."

"Ha. Ha." She tore a leaf from the potted plant next to her and threw it at him. But the greenery only fluttered and fell.

He laughed again. "That was lame. Maybe you ought to try it again, but with a bit more gusto this time."

"Oh, yeah?" She tore off a whole score of leaves, then came over to him and held them over his head. "Who's got gusto now?"

Enjoying their goofy game, he grabbed her wrists, but his attempt at playfulness backfired. Her gaze locked with his, and neither of them moved.

Time could have stood still. The world could have stopped.

He released her wrists, and the leaves drifted from her hands. Some of them floated around his shoulders and the rest got caught in his hair.

"I'm sorry," she said, her apology soft and low.

"It's okay." Still staring at her, he ran his hands through his hair, dusting the leaves away.

"You missed one." She removed it gingerly, dropping it at his feet with the others.

"Thanks." Even as awkward as it was, he liked being touched by her. He liked it too damned much.

She returned to her seat and gazed out at the yard again.

Neither of them spoke until he said, "Maybe it will fizzle out after a while."

She glanced his way. "What?"

"This thing between us. I mean, how long can we keep feeling this way? Months? Years? Every time I come to visit Cody? That would be weird." He didn't see how it could go on.

"I hope it ends."

"Me, too." He tried to relax, to quit thinking about being touched by her. "We'll just do our best to make it stop."

She cocked her head at an angle. "How do we do that?"

"By just being normal around each other, I guess." After a lull in the conversation, he said, "By the way, I meant what I said about taking you and Cody to California. I was even thinking that you could go with me in July."

She looked at him as if he'd just flipped his lid. "Seriously? Considering what we just talked about? You're asking me to take a trip with you?"

"I want Cody to meet my brother, and I don't see how that's going to happen unless you accompany us. I know you'd never agree to let him travel alone with me."

"You're right, I wouldn't. It's too soon for something like that." She had a concerned expression. "So what about your sister? Do you want Cody to meet her, too?"

"I haven't even told him about her yet. I was waiting to ask you how to handle that discussion."

"Just tell him the truth. I've never lied to him about anything, and I certainly don't want you to, either."

"All right. But I don't know if it would be a good idea for him to meet her, not while she's locked up." He leaned forward. "Do you?"

"I don't know, either. We'd have to cross that bridge

when we come to it. But I haven't even agreed that we would go to California with you."

"Will you at least think about it?"

"It would probably be difficult for me to get the time off from work."

"You work for your family."

"That doesn't mean I can just take off on a whim."

"It's over a month away." And he wasn't going to let up until she agreed to consider it. "We can fly instead of drive. That'll save time, and I'll pay for everything and take you and Cody to all of the fun spots. You won't have to do anything but enjoy the experience."

"I don't know. I just—"

"Have you ever even been out of Montana yet? Has Cody? It's crazy not to let our son have a vacation like this."

She fidgeted with her hands, twisting them on her lap. "I'm not used to having to make decisions like this."

"Just promise you'll think about it."

"Okay, I'll think about it." She continued to fidget. "But that doesn't mean you won the battle. If I decide that we're not going, then we're not going."

"Going where?" a young voice said from behind the screen door.

Kade and Bridget turned simultaneously to see Cody standing behind the barrier, still looking half-asleep.

"Nowhere," his mother quickly replied. She got up and went inside. Kade tagged along as she guided the stumbling ten-year-old into the bathroom to brush his teeth.

In no time, the boy changed into his pajamas. Bridget tucked him beneath his covers, and he smiled groggily at his parents. They took turns kissing him good-night, and Kade felt as if he was actually becoming a dad.

Or maybe he was just fooling himself and playing at being one. It was all so new, so different, so unlike anything he'd ever done before, he couldn't really be sure.

Chapter Five

Bridget awakened a half hour before the alarm was set to go off. But just as she closed her eyes, hoping to snooze a little before she had to get up for real, her cell phone rang.

Well, hell.

She reached over and grabbed the blaring device off her nightstand. The caller ID indicated that it was Kade. Of all people. And first thing in the morning.

She answered, trying to sound more awake than she was. "What's going on, Kade?"

"I was wondering if you wanted to work with the barn sour horse today," he replied. "Remember we talked about me coming by sometime this week for a session?"

Actually, she'd forgotten. Between his invitation to California and the impromptu barbecue that was coming up, his offer had slipped her mind.

"Sure," she said, sitting up in bed. "We can work with Misty today." She didn't see any reason in putting it off. The horse needed the training, and Bridget was going to have to get used to seeing Kade, with or without their son present.

"What time should I come by?" he asked.

She glanced at the clock. "Let's say around eight? That will give me time to get Cody up and get him off to school."

"Do you think we could make it a little earlier so I can see him off to school, too?"

"He leaves for the bus stop at seven forty-five. If you're here around seven thirty, then you can spend time with him over breakfast. You can eat with us, if you want."

"I'll be there. But you don't have to feed me. I'm having breakfast right now."

"You are?" Her curiosity was piqued. "Where at?"

"The diner across from the motel."

The greasy spoon where they'd gone together. She pictured him sitting in a small vinyl booth, the ends of his hair still damp from the shower. "What are you having?"

"The special. Eggs, bacon, hash browns and toast. I ordered the eggs overeasy."

She couldn't help but ask, "Did you get enough sugar for your coffee?"

A smile sounded in his voice. "Yes, I did. But you should see the pile of empty packets on the table. Of course, if you were here, it would be twice the mess."

But she wasn't there. She was home in bed, wearing an oversize T-shirt and flower-printed panties and talking to him. Feeling far too intimate, she said, "I should go. I need to get myself together, then get Cody up. Sometimes he can be a grump in the morning."

"Okay. I'll see you in a while. Let the little grump know I'm coming by."

"I will." They ended the call, and she went straight for the shower to cool herself off.

After she washed and dressed and plaited her hair into a single braid, she roused Cody. He whined, wanting to remain in bed, until she told him that his dad was stopping by.

"Really? That's great." He pushed away the covers and lifted his head off the pillow, his night-tousled hair sticking out at odd angles.

She touched his cheek. He had blanket marks like a road map all over it. Between that and his hair, he looked like a young Frankenstein. "You need to get ready now."

He climbed out of bed. "All right."

Leaving him alone, she went into the kitchen and started a pot of coffee. When it was done, she poured it into a "World's Greatest Mom" cup that Cody had given her for Mother's Day. As she added her usual dose of sugar, she thought of Kade. She hoped that wasn't going to happen every time she doctored her coffee, because that would mean thinking about him every morning for the rest of her life. She'd have to give up coffee. And sugar. And everything else that reminded her of him.

Cody entered the room, dressed in his school clothes, and she realized that he was the biggest reminder. All she had to do was look at her son to think about Kade.

"Is Dad here yet?" he asked.

"No. And did you even do your hair? It looks the same as when you first woke up."

"I combed it."

"With what?" She made a quick circular motion. "A blender? Go back and do it again."

He rolled his eyes. "It won't do any good."

"Yes, it will." For a while anyway. By the end of the day, it would be poking up again, but not as bad as it was now. "Go on." She shooed him. "Fix it the right way."

He darted off, and this time when he returned, his hair was tamed with gel.

"Better?" he asked.

"Much." She smiled at how handsome he looked. He was the best and brightest thing in her life. Wanting to pamper him, she said, "I'm going to make you pancakes this morning with bananas and strawberries and whipped cream."

"Do you think I could have one of those breakfast sandwiches we have in the freezer instead? Then I can eat on the porch and wait for Dad to come."

Her heart deflated, but she popped his sandwich into the microwave without letting her emotions show. After the bell dinged, she wrapped the sandwich in a napkin. She removed a juice box from the fridge so he could take that outside, as well.

"Here you go." She handed him the items, hoping her world's-greatest-parent status wasn't dwindling.

"Thanks." He made a mad dash for the door with the food and his backpack. "I see Dad's truck. He just pulled up."

"Perfect timing." She forced an upbeat tone, not wanting him to detect her disappointment.

While he was gone, she made herself toast and jam and stayed at the counter like a mother hen, waiting for her baby chick to return for a hasty goodbye.

But that wasn't what happened. After a short while, Kade came in alone.

"Hey," he said, by way of a greeting. "Cody just left."

Without saying goodbye? He'd never done that before. But his dad had never been here before, either.

"He was certainly excited to see you," she said.

"I was happy to see him, too. We talked about the barbecue and he told me that your grandmother has two potbellied pigs. But he assured me that they were her pets and she wouldn't be roasting them that day." He flashed a proud-papa smile. "Our kid has a cute sense of humor."

She smiled, too, grateful that he appreciated their son's quirky personality. "Sometimes he catches me off guard with the things he says."

"I can see how that would happen." From beneath the summer-straw brim of his Western hat, Kade roamed his gaze over her. "Are you ready for Misty's training?"

She smoothed the front of her blouse, wishing he would stop looking at her as if he wanted to press his body against hers. "Yes, I'm ready."

He kept looking at her. Then finally he said, "Before we go outside and get started, I have a question about Misty's behavior."

She hoped she could respond with a clear head. "What is it?"

"Does she object as soon as you take her away from the barn?"

She nodded. "And the farther we get, the more anxious she becomes." With the same kind of anxiousness Bridget was feeling right now.

"When you first told me about her, you mentioned that she only does this sometimes, and other times she's okay. What's the pattern? For example, does she only object when you take her out alone? Or does she still behave in the same manner when someone is riding the other horse?"

She stopped to think about it. "Misty is fine as long as someone else is with us. But when I'm by myself and taking her out, that's when she acts up." She frowned. "So what do you think is going on?"

"I think it's a case of her being buddy sour."

"Oh, my goodness. I didn't even consider that." *Buddy sour* was a term used for a horse that didn't want to leave his or her pasture buddy. "She wants to stay with Minnie P."

"Horses have two sides to their brains, reactive and thinking. The reactive side comes from their instincts, and their instinct is to stay with the herd. For insecure horses, this is especially true."

"I shouldn't have overlooked the obvious, but I don't take Misty out by herself very often. And since we've only had her for a short time, and I've never had a barn sour or buddy sour horse before, I didn't even look for a pattern."

"It's okay. Now you know better."

"What are you going to have me do to fix it?"

"It depends on what I think is best suited to Misty's temperament. But another thing to consider with a buddy sour horse is the relationship it has with its owner. It's important for Misty to want to be around you, to feel as safe with you as she would with a herd. So I'm also going to address the rapport you have with her and work on that, too."

"I understand." Bridget remembered learning a bit

about equine cognition at the clinic she'd taken from him and the necessity of the human-horse bond.

"No matter what method we use, you need to be patient and consistent. You can't try to rush it."

"I really appreciate this, Kade. I should have done something about it before now." She knew how imperative it was to be in control of a horse at all times. "I'm willing to do whatever is necessary."

"Good. Are you ready to start?"

She nodded, and they left the house and went out to the barn. Kade spent plenty of time with her and Misty, analyzing both of them. But he made it enjoyable, helping her and the mare relax.

After he decided they were ready, he started the exercise by having Bridget take Misty around in a tight circle, where the other horse was out of sight for only a split second. He explained that this should be done every day, increasing the distance, until Misty could walk in a large and calm circle away from her buddy.

Bridget took her cues from Kade, training the mare accordingly. Every so often, though, she would feel fluttery inside. Being in this type of environment with him was stirring a sense of déjà vu, reminding her of the baby-making week they'd spent together. Only this time, they weren't going to end up in bed.

She'd slept with him on the second day, and she would never forget the moment they'd gone back to his motel room. The pounding of her heart. The click of the door as it closed. The warm and sexy way he'd kissed her.

But making love with him was the last thing she should be thinking about, so she did her darnedest to clear her mind.

After the session ended, he said, "You did a good job."

"Thank you." It had gone well, except for her wayward thoughts. "I'll keep working on it."

"And I'll keep coming by to check on your progress. Once you're further along, we can take both horses out and work on separating them on the trail. Then you can advance to taking Misty out by yourself."

"That sounds good." He was the expert, and she would follow his advice.

He dusted his hands on his jeans. "I'm going to take off now, but I was wondering if I could come back this evening. I'd like to take Cody out to dinner and spend a little alone time with him."

"That's fine." She wasn't going to deprive their son of his father's attention. "I'll let him know when he gets home."

"All right, thanks. I'll probably just take him to a drive-through and grab some burgers so we can stay in my truck and talk. I was thinking it might be a good time for me to tell him more about my family and my sister being in prison."

"If you're ready to do that, then I agree that you should."

"Can I also tell him that I invited both of you to come to California with me this summer and that you're considering the trip?"

"Yes, you can tell him." Since she'd already stressed how important she thought it was to be honest with Cody, how could she say no? "But he's probably going to pester the heck out of me once he knows it might be a possibility."

Kade shot her a buoyant smile. "That's the idea."

"So I gathered." Caught in the web of his appeal, she smiled, too. She was beginning to like Kade Quinn as much as she had the first moment she'd met him, making every second that he was around that much sweeter. And scarier. And everything else that went with it.

Kade and Cody kicked back in the parking lot of the drive-through, munching on cheeseburgers, fries and milk shakes.

"So your sister did something bad?" the boy asked, in response to Kade telling him Meagan was in prison.

"She stole money from the place where she worked."

"Like out of a cash register or something?"

"No. She didn't have a job like that. She worked for an accountant and she tampered with the books, so she was able to take money from other people's bank accounts and keep it for herself."

Cody wiped a smear of ketchup from his mouth. "Why did she do that?"

"Because she got greedy, and now she's suffering the consequences." Meagan had been trying to live the high life with her loser ex-boyfriend, but Kade refrained from stating it that way. "I haven't seen her since before she got arrested, but my brother said that she's sorry for what she did. She's sad, too, because she has a baby daughter named Ivy who she can't take care of until she gets released. And she won't be out for almost two years."

"Is her husband taking care of the baby?"

"No. My brother is. Meagan isn't married."

"Is the dad even around?"

"Yes, but he isn't involved with the baby."

"Is he a bad person?"

Damn, Kade thought. He was trying to tread lightly about this. "Yes, you could say that." The jerk had encouraged Meagan to take the money, and then ditched her when she got caught, even after he'd discovered she was pregnant. "He just isn't interested in his daughter."

"How come so many guys aren't interested in their kids?"

Kade looked into his son's eyes and saw his concern. "I have no idea. But I won't do that to you."

"I wish you could move here."

A stream of guilt ran through his blood. A shot of panic, too. He couldn't imagine staying in one spot for the rest of his life. "Even if I lived here, I'd still be traveling, so you wouldn't see me any more often than if I came to visit. So how about if I just visit when I can, and we'll make the most of being able to see each other when I'm here?"

"Okay," Cody replied. Then he continued by saying, "I was hoping that if you lived here, you'd be around more. But I already figured that you lived on the road like my mom said her dad used to do."

Kade didn't like the comparison, but he couldn't deny the similarity. "It doesn't make sense for me to have my own home. I go from place to place, staying wherever I'm working. A lot of my clients put me up at their ranches when I'm working for them." He'd been offered permanent positions, but he'd always refused, wanting to be free to move on. "If they don't provide boarding, then I'll rent a cabin or a lodge, like I'm going to do while I'm here. If it's a really short job, I'll just crash at a motel."

"What about your horses? Where do they stay when you don't bring them with you?"

"I don't have horses of my own. I used to, but I don't anymore. It's easier to travel without having to worry about them."

Cody all but gaped at him. "That's weird."

"What? A horse trainer with no horses? I don't need my own, not when I'm spending so much time with everyone else's."

"I couldn't do what you do. I like having a home and horses and my own stuff."

"I have stuff. Just not that much of it. I do have some belongings in storage in California, though, where my mom's things are stored. She died a few years ago. I also had another sister who passed away when she was six months old. That was a sad time for my family." His mother had nearly had a breakdown over it.

"What about your dad? Is he still around?"

"Yes, but I stopped talking to him or seeing him when I was in my twenties. Meagan and Tanner don't have anything to do with him, either. He treated us badly." Kade hated that the conversation kept coming back to crummy fathers, but it was what it was. "He traveled a lot for his work, too. But whenever he came home, he made our lives miserable."

"Did he hit you?" Cody asked.

The question in itself packed a punch, but Kade tried not to tense. "Not when I was a kid. We got in a fight once when I was older."

"That must have been awful."

"It was." They'd pounded each other bloody, with no one else around to stop it. By then, Kade's parents were divorced and his siblings were living with their mom. "I shouldn't have even bothered to visit him that day." To soften the discussion, he said, "But I'm lucky that I have my brother. We don't see each other that often, but we're still close. You're going to like your uncle Tanner. He's a great guy. He's engaged to a sweet girl, too. She's helping him take care of Meagan's baby."

"How am I ever going to meet them, with them being so far away?" The boy shrugged. "I guess we could video chat."

"Yes, you could do that. But I have a better idea." Which was when the topic of conversation segued seamlessly into the vacation he'd proposed to Bridget. "I invited you and your mom to go to California with me in July. She isn't sure about it, though, so we're going to have to convince her to agree."

"Oh, man." Cody bounced in his seat. "I'm going to bug her every day till she says yes."

"She said that you'd start pestering her. So do your best to make her listen."

"I will, Dad. I'll drive her crazy with it."

Kade chuckled. "That's the spirit. California or bust."

"Heck, yeah. Can we go to Disneyland and Hollywood and to the beach, where people are surfing and stuff?"

"Absolutely. I already told your mom we could hit all the fun spots."

"I want to go so bad I can taste it." To prove his point, Cody polished off his burger with one big messy bite and washed it down with a swig of his shake.

Kade joined him, wolfing the rest of his burger down, too. Afterward, they smiled, enjoying the goofy bond.

In the silence that followed, Cody asked, "Will I get to meet your sister?"

"Do you want to meet her?"

"Sure. I don't think it would be right for me to ignore her 'cause she did something bad. She's still my aunt."

"That's nice. I appreciate that. But it would mean taking you to visit her at prison, and your mom and I aren't sure about that."

"It wouldn't bother me going to see her there. Really, I wouldn't mind."

"We'll have to see how it goes." But first they needed to convince Bridget how truly important this trip was.

Chapter Six

Bridget glanced around the barbecue. About twenty-five people were in attendance, scattered in lawn chairs and at patio tables and wherever else they found a spot. The food had already been served, and at this stage of the gathering the guests were either going back for seconds or just hanging out and talking. Bridget and Maura Kinney, her closest and most loyal friend, stood in the background, a short distance from the main activity.

They'd gone to high school together, and now they were both thirty-one-year-old moms. Maura, a pixie-haired brunette with a rosy complexion, was seven months pregnant with her second child. At the moment she was balancing Sadie Lynn, her firstborn, a sweet and squirming toddler, against her hip. Bridget's son was dashing around the party with his friends, dumping cups of ice on each other's heads and pealing with boyish laughter.

"Kade is even hotter in person than I expected him to be," Maura said as she gazed at him from across Grandma's grassy yard. "And dang if doesn't keep looking your way."

Yes, he kept stealing glances at Bridget. But he was also sitting next to her grandma in a lawn chair, engaged in a cozy conversation. "Having him here hasn't been easy."

"No doubt." Maura turned toward Bridget. "Not with the way he's making you drool."

"I'm not drooling."

"You sure about that?"

Just in case, she checked the corners of her lips. Thankfully, they were dry.

"He seems like he's going to be a good dad." Maura smoothed her daughter's sundress, stopping it from riding up past her diapered bottom and ruffled bloomers. "I noticed how attentive he is with Cody. I saw them together earlier, and how well they interact with each other."

"They're definitely getting close, and I'm glad it's working in Cody's favor." Bridget went ahead and spilled her insecurities. "But sometimes it's tough for me with the way he worships Kade. It makes me feel left out. But I understand how new and intoxicating it is for both of them, so I keep telling myself not to feel that way. Besides, I'm beginning to really like Kade again, too."

Maura gave her daughter's dress another gentle tug. "He does seem rather irresistible."

"You have no idea. He's helping me train one of our horses, and just knowing that he's going to be popping in to check on my progress is exciting. I want to be around him. But it's scary, too."

"So you're still afraid that Kade might morph into a clone of your father?"

"Yes, I am. And I don't know what it's going to take to make me stop feeling that way."

"Maybe you just need more time."

Or maybe Kade needed to be the kind of man who didn't roam from place to place like her dad. "He invited Cody and me to go to California with him to meet his family. He offered to pay for the whole trip and take us sightseeing."

"Then, by all means, you should go. Who gets a free trip like that?"

"Cody is campaigning for it. Ever since Kade told him, it's all I've been hearing about. California this and California that. If I say no, I'm going to be the biggest ogre who ever lived."

"So just think of how much fun it'll be for you jetting off with a guy like Kade. You might as well make the most of it."

Bridget tried to taper her friend's enthusiasm. "He only asked me to go because I won't let him take Cody by himself. I doubt he would have invited me otherwise."

"But what about the chemistry between the two of you? That has to count for something."

"We're both hoping it will fizzle out."

"I can see how complicated that must be."

"When he disappeared the first time, I assumed that I'd never see him again. And now's he's back, this sexy temptation I'm struggling to resist."

"Going to California with him still sounds better than staying here and watching the grass grow."

Bridget reached for Sadie Lynn, taking the toddler in her arms. If she'd fallen for a homebound man and married him, she would've had more kids by now. "My life isn't that boring."

"Really? When's the last time you did something exciting? Or better yet, what's the most exciting thing you've ever done? From what I recall, it was the week you climbed into bed with Kade."

She hated that Maura was right. "I'm not going to dignify that with a response."

"Why? Because I hit the nail on the head?"

Trapped with the truth, Bridget glanced over at Kade again. He was still engaged in conversation with her grandma, with the brim of his hat dipping low on his forehead. "I wonder what they're talking about."

"Heaven only knows. But it looks as if they're getting along just fine. I noticed that your mom barely said anything to him, though, other than a polite 'How do you do?' when they first met."

"I noticed that, too. But I figured that was how she was going to react to him. It's definitely going to take some time for her to trust him."

"Do you think she ever really will? Or do you think she'll always be waiting for the other shoe to drop?"

"I don't know." Bridget couldn't even answer that question for herself. "My dad came around for seven years before he ditched us. If Kade does that to our son seven years from now, Cody will be in his last year of high school. Can you imagine how devastating that would be?"

"You shouldn't even be making those types of comparisons."

"No, I shouldn't." But those fears continued to haunt her. She jiggled Sadie Lynn and made the little girl smile. "I envy you, Maura."

"Me? With this big belly? Seriously, girl, wouldn't you rather be flying off to California in a bikini?"

Bridget laughed a little. "I wouldn't be flying there in a bikini. I'd be properly dressed, I assure you."

Maura grinned, looking like the pregnant pixie she was. "So does that mean you're going to go?"

"I don't know what it means." She sneaked another peek at Kade, and he glanced up and met her gaze at the very same time, sending her uncertainty into an even deeper tailspin.

Kade couldn't seem to tear his gaze away from Bridget's, even from across the crowded yard. Not until her grandmother cleared her throat, deliberately drawing his attention back to her.

"My granddaughter is a beautiful young lady," she said.

"Yes, she is. But nothing is going to happen between us."

"It already happened, my dear boy. Nearly eleven years ago."

He shook his head. "I meant that nothing was going to happen now."

"So you're going to be around Bridget year after year, visiting your son, and you think that you're going to be able to keep your hands off her? And she's going to be able to control her hotsy doodles for you?"

Hotsy doodles? He swigged his soda to keep from

laughing. Or cringing. Or whatever it was he was supposed to be feeling, discussing his nonexistent sex life with an outspoken senior.

In addition to her feisty nature, she also had silver hair that she wore like a mantle, long bony fingers and blue eyes that twinkled when she talked. Her name was Edith, but she'd told him that he could call her Grandma since that was how he would come to know her.

"So, do you?" she asked, pressing him to answer.

"Yes, I do."

"Well, good luck with that. Because I'd say within the sight of a month, you two will be kissing the devil out of each other and praying for mercy."

"Gee, thanks for trusting us to behave."

"I just call them like I see them." Grandma sipped her soda. Then she said, "I like you, Kade. I think Tom would have liked you, too."

Tom, he'd already learned, was her deceased husband. "Thank you for saying that. I like you, as well. And I'm sorry for your loss."

Her voice rattled a little. "We were married for fifty wonderful years."

Kade couldn't imagine being married, let alone for half a century. "That's a hell of an accomplishment."

"Yes, it is, and I'm proud of it." She raised her cola, saluting herself and the man she'd lost. "Tom and I were a team."

"My parents had a lousy marriage. There was always tension in our household. Or sadness. Or both. It affected me in ways that I still feel. My brother and sister still feel it, too. We never understood why our mother took the divorce so hard. She should have been glad to be rid of our old man."

"Some women don't know when to let go. Nora was like that."

Ah, yes, Bridget's mom. He wasn't sure what to make of her, other than noticing her giving him the cold shoulder. "Who was Bridget's dad?"

"His name was Lance Hooper. He was a nice-looking chap, about average height with a stocky build and light brown hair. He was a heck of salesman, with a friendly nature. But he needed his time alone, that's for sure."

"How much do you know about him?"

"About his past, you mean? Lance didn't have a good upbringing. His mama was a drinker, always hitting the bars and bringing home men. He didn't know who his daddy was, and he said he didn't care because he figured it was probably just some loser who'd bought his mom a drink. Lance ran away from home when he was a teenager, and by the time Nora met him, he was used to running. That's why he could only handle being around her and Bridget in small doses. Plus, he wasn't in love with Nora, and he knew she was waiting around for him to marry her."

Kade admitted how he felt. "I understand Lance's need to be free. Not everyone is wired to settle down. But even if he didn't want to be with Nora, he shouldn't have walked away from Bridget."

"I agree. But I suspect that he was concerned that if he kept seeing Bridget, he would have to keep seeing Nora, too. He was never really able to separate them. They were so much alike, mother and daughter, hanging on his every word, desperate for him to be a bigger part of their lives."

Kade went quiet, listening to the rest of Grandma's tale.

"At first he tried to cope with the pressure by visiting less frequently. And then he finally came to the conclusion that the only way to be free was to leave and not come back." She paused, her expression tight. "Tom wanted to drag his sorry ass back here and force him to marry our daughter. He hated how Lance was always coming and going and leaving Nora and Bridget in the lurch. Now me, I rather liked him, in spite of his faults."

"You didn't blame him for leaving?"

"It upset me that he hurt my girls. But I also came to the conclusion that they were better off without him. I think maybe that's how Lance saw it, too. That in some warped way he thought he was giving them a chance to find someone else. A man who would actually marry Nora and become the kind of father Bridget needed."

"But nothing like that ever happened."

"No." Grandma sighed. "Nothing did."

"And now here I am, serving as a reminder of the pain Lance caused." Kade glanced at Nora, who was sitting at a patio table on the other side of the yard, with her back to him. "I appreciate that you're not lumping me together with Lance and the choices he made, the way Nora and Bridget are."

"I'm not going to judge you by what he did. I never agreed with Bridget's reason for not telling you about Cody. I understand that she was hurt that you never called her and fearful that you were too much like her daddy, but you had a right to know about your son."

"I'm glad that I know about him now. He's an amazing kid."

She smiled. "He most certainly is."

Kade considered Cody's relationship with the women in his family. "What does he call Bridget's mom to distinguish her from you? You're not both Grandma to him, are you?"

"No. She's Nana Nora. He likes using her name because he thinks it sounds good with *nana*."

"Do they spend a lot of time together?"

"Yes, very much so. He spends as much time with her as he does with me. We're a tight-knit group."

Both sets of Kade's grandparents had died a long time ago. He didn't have any memories of them. "My mom was the one who held us kids together. But sometimes she could be overly emotional, too."

"Cody told me that you offered to take him and Bridget to California to meet your brother and his fiancée."

"Did he tell you about my sister?"

She nodded. "I don't have any reservations about him meeting her."

"I think Cody is more comfortable about going to the prison than I am."

"Then, you should definitely take him with you, if you can. It'll be nice for you to have your son there, helping you relax. I think it will be nice for him, too, being your support system. It'll boost his confidence to know that his daddy needs him. Bridget never got that from her father."

Kade noticed that Bridget's pregnant friend was waddling off with her kid and heading back over to her husband, leaving Bridget alone. It made Bridget seem like a lost soul, even at a party surrounded by her peers. He could only assume she was like that when she was little, too. "Her dad really did a number on her."

"Yes, he did. But he was obviously screwed up in his own way. No one is perfect." Grandma glanced in

Bridget's direction. "I suspect that she wanted to take road trips with her daddy, but he never invited her to go along. I think it would be good for her to get away with you and Cody."

"Bridget said that it might be difficult for her to get the time off from work."

Grandma waved away his comment. "That's nonsense. I can cover for her. I'm retired now, but I helped run that business for years. She can't use that as an excuse."

"Would you mind if I went over and talked to her?"

"Of course not. Go right ahead. I've been monopolizing you long enough, and there are other guests I should be chatting with."

"Thank you." He got up to leave. "I really appreciate how kind you've been to me."

He headed toward Bridget, and as soon she saw him coming, he noticed her anxious behavior: the way she shifted her feet, the manner in which she tucked her hands into the back pockets of her jeans.

He was anxious, too. But he figured it was because of Grandma's opinion about him and Bridget not having any restraint. Would they really be kissing and touching before the summer was through?

He approached her and asked the most generic question he could think of. "Are you enjoying the barbecue?"

"Yes, it's nice." She kept her hands in her back pockets. "How about you?"

"It's a great bunch of people." He'd been introduced to everyone, and aside from Nora, they all seemed receptive to him. But he supposed that Bridget's mom couldn't look at him without thinking of Lance. "I really like your grandma. But I knew I would. She's been my ally from the start." He politely inquired, "Can I get you a drink or anything?"

"No, thanks. I've had plenty to eat and drink."

He stalled for a second, trying to come up with something else to say. Then he opted for, "Your grandmother thinks the California trip would be good for you."

"My friend Maura thinks so, too."

"I'm glad she agrees." He appreciated the support. He would take whatever he could get from whoever was willing to see things his way. "Maybe you should just go for it."

Bridget didn't give in. "I'm not ready to make that decision."

He forged on. He'd never been easily deterred, not when he wanted something. "Your grandmother approves of Cody going to the prison to meet Meagan."

"She's very open-minded. She's always been like that. I think Cody gets his personality from her."

"They do seem a lot alike."

"They can both drive me a little crazy."

Kade intended to drive her down his path, too. "I'm going to ask Meagan to send the necessary forms so you and Cody will be able to visit her, just in case you agree to take the trip. You'd just have to fill out the paperwork and mail it back so they can do a background check on you."

She furrowed her brows. "Did you already have them do yours?"

"Yes. I did it a while ago." Even if he hadn't seen his sister yet. "So what's your main concern about the trip? Why do you need more time to decide?"

"It just seems like a major thing to travel with you. Or to travel at all. And it might be awkward for me meeting your brother and his fiancée. Cody is your son, but I'm just the girl you spent time with at a motel."

"You're way more than that. You're Cody's mother, and they're going to see what a terrific job you're doing of raising him. They're going to respect you for that, especially now that they've become surrogate parents to Meagan's baby."

"Just give me a few more days to think about it."

"Okay." He went for a smile. "But if you say no, Cody and I will keep bugging you till you say yes."

"So you both keep saying." A smile worked its way across her lips, too. "Like father, like son." She finally removed her hands from her pockets. "Have you found another place to stay, besides the motel?"

"Actually, I did. It's a cabin near the river, with a fire pit in the backyard. I'll be moving into it on Monday. Maybe you and Cody can come by and see it after you get off work that day?"

"Sure, we can do that."

"Great. We can have a bonfire and roast marshmallows. Maybe we can discuss the time capsule, too, and figure out what items you and I are going to put in it. Cody is working so hard on his comic, and we haven't come up with anything yet."

"Yes, we can discuss that, as well. Speaking of Cody..." She motioned to their son, who was running around the barbecue with his friends, all of them soaked to the gills. "I better get some towels. It looks like the ice fight the kids were having turned into a full-blown water fight."

Kade thought it looked like fun, making him wish the adults could join in. Then again, he'd gotten wet with Bridget before. They'd splashed in the shower, so playing in the water with her probably wasn't a good idea. Not if it stirred those old memories. He didn't need to be tempted by her any more than he already was.

Chapter Seven

The cabin Kade rented was warm and inviting, fully furnished with a compact kitchen, a stone fireplace and rugged oak beams. Bridget thought it suited him.

"Where's the bedroom?" Cody asked.

"It doesn't have one," Kade replied. "This couch turns into a bed."

Bridget glanced at the puffy brown sofa in question and imagined Kade sleeping there. When she'd stayed with him in the motel, he'd slept naked. She'd gone bare then, too, even though she normally wore pajamas. She didn't know if he wore anything to bed when he was alone. Not that she should be thinking about him in a state of undress. She knew better than to let her mind wander in that direction.

"We brought marshmallows in case you needed more," she said, holding up the supermarket bag in her hand. "They're the jumbo kind."

Kade took them from her. "That's the kind I got, too. But I appreciate having extra. We can stuff ourselves silly."

"At Christmastime we make snowmen out of the smaller ones," Cody said. "First we melt caramel and dip the bottoms of some marshmallows into it. Then we place them on gingersnap cookies. After that, we build the rest of the snowmen from more marshmallows and use icing to hold them together."

Kade smiled. "That's sounds cute."

"It is. We use straight pretzels for their arms and candy sprinkles for their faces. Oh, and gumdrops for their hats. That's my favorite part, besides giving them to our neighbors." The eager ten-year-old looked up at him. "Are you going to visit next Christmas?"

"I will if it's okay with your mom." Kade shifted toward Bridget, catching her gaze. "But that's still quite a ways off."

"Yes, it is." She didn't want to think about making future plans. She was just trying to get through each day. "We'll have to figure that out when the time gets closer."

"Where do you usually go for Christmas?" Cody asked his dad, keeping the conversation going.

"It depends. Sometimes I see my family. Other times I hang out with friends or clients who invite me to their houses. But there have been plenty of times that I've been alone, too."

Cody frowned. So did Bridget. She couldn't fathom being alone during the holidays. But apparently Kade could.

Cody said, "We always have Christmas Eve at our house and Mom lets me open one present. Then in the morning, I get to open the rest of them and we go to Grandma's for dinner. Nana Nora goes there, too. She brings lots of presents and helps with the meal. It was weird last year because Grandpa wasn't around anymore. He always watched Christmas movies with me, and we both wore Santa hats. He already had a white beard, so his hat looked really good on him."

"I can see how much you miss him," Kade said.

"If you come next Christmas, maybe you can wear a hat and watch movies with me."

"I'd love to do that. But I doubt I'd look as good in the hat as your grandpa."

Cody grinned. "We could get you a fake beard."

Kade laughed and scratched his chin. "No doubt it would be better than anything I could ever grow. All I ever seem to manage is a bit of stubble."

Bridget remembered how sexy he looked after a few days of not shaving. She recalled how rough his whiskers felt against her bare skin, too. To keep from getting dreamy, she asked, "Should we get the bonfire and marshmallows going?"

Kade replied, "I couldn't find any skewers in the kitchen, but I figured we could use wire coat hangers. There are some in here." He opened a tall, sturdy armoire where his clothes were hanging.

His wardrobe consisted of mostly jeans, T-shirts and Western shirts. Bridget did spot a dinner jacket and slacks, though. His underwear was probably tucked away in the drawer at the bottom of the cabinet. From what she recalled, he favored boxer briefs.

While Bridget cleared her thoughts, Cody reshaped the hangers and Kade started the bonfire. Immersed in the moment, she sat in a chair and glanced up at the sky.

The sun was setting, creating a maroon haze across the clouds. She took solace in the picturesque view, with its mountain backdrop.

As they gathered around the fire, roasting marshmallows, the toasty atmosphere made them seem like a family. But they weren't, and she wasn't going to fool herself into believing that they were.

Kade asked her, "Have you decided on what you're going to put in the time capsule?"

"Yes." She'd thought long and hard about it, trying to come up with things that made sense. "There are two items I'm going to use. First, I'm going to make a copy of Cody's birth certificate. I thought that would be a good way to identify us, with everyone's names being on it."

"I'm on it, too?" Kade asked.

She nodded. "You're listed as the father." She wouldn't have put *unknown* or left that area blank. To her, that would have been cheating their child out of the truth. "I didn't know your middle name, though. So it just says Kade Quinn."

"My middle name is Minninnewah. It means Wild Wind or Whirlwind in Cheyenne. My mother chose it because I moved around so much in her belly. She said I was like a whirlwind spinning in her womb."

"It's definitely right for you," Bridget said. It fit him perfectly, even now, with the way he moved through life, going from place to place. "Do Tanner and Meagan have Cheyenne names, too?"

"No. My dad didn't like mine, so he told her not to do it again. I don't think he liked my first name, either. Or Tanner's or Meagan's. Or Ella's, for that matter. Nothing about us pleased him."

"Is Ella your sister who died?"

He nodded. "Meagan calls her an angel. I try to think of her that way, too." He softly asked, "How did you come up with Cody's name?"

Her stupid heart went pitter-patter, affected by the warmth in his eyes. "I named him after Buffalo Bill Cody. He's my favorite Western historical character."

"What about Cody's middle name? How does that factor into it?"

"Colton? I just thought it sounded good with his first name."

"It does. I like it." He smiled at their son, and the boy returned his father's affection with a smile of his own.

Bridget noticed how quiet Cody was being tonight, eating his third helping of marshmallows and listening to his parents talk.

Kade searched her gaze. "What's your middle name?"

Her heart fluttered once again. "Lauren."

He kept watching her. "Bridget Lauren Wells. That's pretty."

"Thank you." She struggled not to stare back at him, to get more mesmerized than she already was. He looked far too handsome by the firelight.

"What's the second item you're going to put in the time capsule?" he asked.

"It's a toy necklace." Something she was ready to part with now that Kade was here. "You got it for me on one of the days we were together. It came out of a gumball machine."

"Oh, wow." He sounded surprised. "You still have that?"

"Yes." She'd been storing it in a box in her closet

with other mementos from her past. "I didn't know if you'd remember it."

"I totally do. We were in a discount store, just looking around, and you wanted bubble gum on the way out. Then you got obsessed with the necklace, so I tried to get it for you. But I ran out of change, so I went back for more. I kept trying until the necklace finally popped out."

"You spent at least forty dollars in quarters, maybe even more. I wanted the necklace so badly because I had one similar to it when I was a kid."

"Doesn't it have hearts or something on it?"

"Yes, along with green stones that look like emeralds. When I was little, I used to pose in front of the mirror with the original one and pretend the gems were real. It was after my dad left, and I needed to cheer myself up. Then I broke it one day and cried like a baby. That's why the one you gave me was so special and why I kept it all these years. It's still in the plastic container it came in."

"I had no idea why it was so important to you. You never told me any of this before." Kade seemed concerned. "Are you sure you want to bury the necklace in the time capsule?"

"Yes." She was certain. "It seems like the best place for it to be."

Cody remained quiet for a few more minutes. Then he asked his father, "What are you going to put in the capsule?"

Kade replied, "I figured that I'd write a note, explaining who I am and that I just met my amazing kid for the first time."

Their son basked in the compliment. "Thanks, Dad. Are you going to mention Mom in the note?"

Kade looked at Bridget again. "Yes, of course. She's a major part of this."

She couldn't imagine how he was going to describe his association with her. "Are you going to let us read the note?"

"Actually, I was thinking of keeping it sealed."

"So whoever opens our time capsule can be the first to read it?" Cody asked.

Kade nodded. "Yes, that's exactly why."

Bridget would prefer to read it herself. But she couldn't stop him from keeping it private. He had a right to decide what felt right to him. But she wished it wasn't going to be so secretive.

"It sounds mysterious," she said.

"It won't be once someone opens it."

It most definitely was to her. "Are you going to put anything else in the capsule?"

"Besides the note? No, but I'd like for the three of us to take some pictures for it. We can start tonight with a bonfire selfie."

Cody said, "That's a great idea. Then the people who open the capsule will be able to see us and compare us to the comic I'm doing."

"They sure can." Kade got up and moved his chair beside Bridget's. Cody was on her other side. Kade removed his cell phone from his pocket, and they huddled in close.

They smiled for the camera, and he snapped the picture. He did a few more, and they laughed once they checked them out because the flash highlighted the ring of marshmallow goo around Cody's mouth. He'd eaten almost an entire bag by himself.

After the photo session, Kade stayed right where he was, far too close to Bridget. The sun was completely gone now, the moon slipping up from behind the trees.

He leaned even closer, his voice lightly audible. "So what's the verdict?"

She spoke in a hushed tone, too. "About what?"

"California."

At the barbecue she'd told him that she needed a few more days to consider it, but she couldn't concentrate right now, not with how close he was. "I don't know."

"Come on, say you'll go."

Just as she considered closing her eyes and shutting him out, Cody asked, "What are you guys whispering about?"

Kade replied, "I'm trying to convince your mom to take the California plunge." He tugged gently on her braid. "But she's being stubborn."

Cody stood up and gave her a pleading look. "Please, Mom. Just agree to take the trip. It's the most important thing in the world to me, and waiting around for you to decide is nerve-racking."

She was on pins and needles, too, especially with the way Kade was making her feel. But she couldn't keep Cody hanging any longer. He deserved an answer. So she gave him the one he wanted to hear. "Okay. We can go. All of us. Together."

Cody let out a piercing whoop and dived straight into her arms. In the midst of the excitement, she was nearly knocked out of her seat and onto Kade's lap. He caught her before she fell and thanked her for saying yes, his breath warm against her ear.

God help her, she thought.

When she went to bed later that night, all she could think about was saying yes to him.

Over and over again.

On Tuesday morning, Kade pressed the buzzer beside Bridget's door. He hadn't called ahead, but he'd timed it so that he would be able to see her and Cody before they left for work and school.

Bridget answered, wearing a pair of blue-and-white pajamas. She stared uncomprehendingly at him. Then she stated the obvious. "I'm not dressed yet."

"Sorry." He tried not to think about the feminine curves hidden beneath her pinstriped pj's. Or how wholesome she looked in them. "I thought you'd be ready by now."

"I don't have to be to work until noon, so I wasn't in a hurry to get dressed. Are you here to see Cody?"

"I was hoping to talk to both of you." He had a proposition that was burning a hole in his head. "It won't take long."

"Then, come in." She stepped away from the door. "Cody is in his room. He already had breakfast, so he's working on his comic, squeezing in a little extra time whenever he can get it."

Kade followed her down the hall, and she tapped lightly on their son's partially open door. "Honey, your dad is here. He wants to talk to us."

As always, Cody was happy to see Kade. It made him feel better about the intrusion. Bridget was still being shy. But he figured that she was uncomfortable about getting caught in her pajamas by the guy who'd once shared a bed with her. With each day that passed, the heat between them kept getting stronger.

But as the three of them gathered in Cody's room, Kade cleared the temptation from his mind and said, "I talked to Tanner this morning and told him that you're both coming to California with me. He's thrilled that he'll get to meet you. I also told him about the time capsule, and he thought it was a brilliant idea. Now he wants to do one for himself, his fiancée and baby Ivy. Oh, and for Meagan, too. He's going to put all of their stuff in one capsule, like we're doing with ours."

"Really?" Cody sounded intrigued. He sat at his desk, surrounded by art supplies, the comic book open to a page that depicted his young, vibrant self in superhero gear. "Where are they going to bury theirs?"

"That's what I wanted to run past you. Tanner suggested that we bury ours in the same spot as theirs, which would be at his stables. He offered to have a ceremony on the day we bury them. A lot of families do that."

"That sounds fun." Cody closed his pencil box. "Doesn't it, Mom?"

She quietly replied, "I'm okay with whatever you want to do. I just want this trip to make you happy."

"It is," Cody said, springing in his seat. "I can't wait to go."

Kade smiled, glad that Cody was pleased. He also appreciated that Bridget was allowing it to happen. "I'm going to order a plaque with everyone's names on it to mark the spot where we bury the capsules."

"It sounds so official." Cody clapped his hands together. "I love it, Dad. I totally do."

"Thank you. I think it's going to be a meaningful

experience." Kade certainly wanted it to be as special as possible. "I'm looking forward to it."

Cody's face took on a serious expression. "Do you think I could put something of Grandpa's in our capsule? If we're going to have a ceremony and a plaque, it would be nice if I could make Grandpa a part of it."

"Of course you can do that." Kade thought it was a fitting tribute for the man who'd helped raise Cody. "If we're going to include people who passed, I can choose something for my mother and Ella. Mom would definitely approve of us doing this, and Ella's life was so short, it would bring even more meaning to who she was." Memories of his angel-sister floated to the surface. "I didn't see Ella that much since I was away at college. But the last time I came home to visit before she died, she was like a little monkey, tugging at my shirt and knocking my hat off my head. She had the cutest smile. Her first two bottom teeth had just come in."

"Do you have any pictures of her?" Cody asked.

"Not on me. But there are old photos in storage. I can show them to you when we get to California." Kade considered the impending ceremony. "We'll honor our family members who died. But we won't make it sad. It'll be a happy occasion."

Cody remarked, "That sounds good to me. I don't want it to be like a funeral."

"Me, neither," Kade said. "It needs to be uplifting."

"For sure." Cody reached for his backpack, preparing to go off to school. "So what are you going to do today, Dad? Do you have anything going on?"

"I haven't made any plans for later. But I was going to check on Misty while I'm here to see how her training is coming along." He turned to Bridget. "If it isn't a problem for you."

"That's fine. I was planning on working with Misty this morning, too." Her gaze locked onto his. "But I need some time to get myself together."

"Should we meet at the barn?" he asked, giving her the opportunity to get dressed without him being in the house. He was feeling the heat, too. She looked far too kissable in the morning light. "I can saddle Misty for you."

She took him up on his offer, and another wave of awkward eye contact passed before they both said goodbye to their son. Cody didn't seem to notice. The ten-year-old dashed off with a wave and a smile, leaving his parents to fend for themselves.

After Kade went outside, Bridget rushed to get ready, and then realized she'd misbuttoned her blouse. Thank goodness she'd caught it. The last thing she needed was to see Kade with her clothes askew. It was bad enough that she'd answered the door in her pajamas, after a night of tossing and turning and thinking about him.

She checked her reflection one last time. She even smoothed the zipper on her jeans, making sure she hadn't left it open after tucking in the tails of her blouse.

With a shaky sense of confidence, she advanced to the backyard. And there he was, her living, breathing fantasy, looking like the ultimate cowboy, holding on to Misty's reins. The horse waited patiently, behaving beautifully for him.

Bridget took the reins and climbed in the saddle. She began the exercise, showing him how far Misty had come.

"She's doing great," he said.

Yes, the horse was responding. But all Bridget felt was anxiety over being watched by Kade. She continued the lesson, forcing herself to keep going.

But each time she passed him, she got more nervous. She was chock-full of butterflies, until he started making Dudley Do-Right faces at her, urging her to relax. She even laughed at his antics.

"You're incorrigible," she said, glad that her composure had been restored.

He motioned for her to widen the circle. "That's why I get the big bucks."

"You're doing this for free, smarty."

"Are you kidding? I'm going to send you a big whopping bill later."

They joked the entire time. Bridget had to admit, she was charmed by the father of her child. She still had concerns about traveling with him, but short of breaking Cody's heart, she couldn't bail out on the trip. She was locked in to California, no matter what it entailed.

When the session was over, she turned Misty back over to Kade. "Will you take her to the barn?"

"What? Like your own personal groom? Yes, I can do that." He looked Bridget straight in the eye; there was a roguish gleam in his. "But if you don't pay the bill, I'm taking it out of your hide."

Her pulse jumped at the thought. "As if I'm going to let you anywhere near my hide."

"You could if you wanted to."

She stopped the flirtation before it went too far. This wasn't a discussion they should be having. "We both know better."

"Yeah, we do." He led Misty away without saying anything else.

But a short time later, he returned and said, "Your grandmother thinks that within a month's time, you and I are going to be kissing the devil out of each other and praying for mercy."

Heaven forbid. Bridget had enough on her plate without adding that to the mix. "My grandmother needs to keep her opinions to herself."

"It's too late for that. She also said that you have the hotsy doodles for me." He bit down on his lip as if he was trying to keep from laughing.

"That's not funny."

"Yes, it is. And she's right. You do."

"Cut it out, Kade." She gave him a sturdy shove, using all her might, but it didn't do any good. He didn't even rock back on his heels.

He stood as tall and straight as a tree, his boots planted firmly on the ground. "You know you want to kiss me, Bridget."

"Not any more than you want to kiss me."

He raised his eyebrows. "Is that a challenge?"

Was it? "No," she said. "And you'd better go now." Before she lost her senses and put her mouth against his.

"All right. But I'm coming back on your next day off."

"What for?"

"For us to take both horses out. I think Misty's ready for a trail session."

"It's not too soon for that?"

"I'm pretty sure she can handle it." His smile went rough. "As long as you can."

Now who was challenging whom? "I can handle it just fine."

"So can I. Nothing is going to happen on my end," he added as he walked away, leaving her in the middle of the yard.

"It's not going to happen on mine, either," she called back, making darned sure that he heard her. Bridget wasn't going to be the weak link.

Even if she was already praying for mercy.

Chapter Eight

Bridget's next day off was at the end of the week. Kade came by and they took the horses out on the trail. They separated Misty from her buddy for a small portion of the ride, and then got the horses back together for the duration of the outing, which meant that Bridget remained in Kade's company, too.

They rode along the water, enjoying the beauty of Flower River. She tried not to think about the kiss that they'd both insisted wasn't going to happen. But it was tough keeping those desires at bay, especially when they stopped to picnic with a blanket draped on the ground.

"This is nature at its finest," Kade said as he unwrapped one of the roast-beef sandwiches she'd made. "It's even prettier than the trails near the cabin."

Bridget nibbled on cheese and crackers, keeping her mouth busy. "I love it here, too." She glanced out into the distance, where a recreational ranch was located. "It's where the other half lives."

"It certainly has a lot to offer. For someone who has the need to put down roots," he added.

Which left him out, obviously. "So do you have your next job lined up? When are you leaving?"

He furrowed his brow. "Are you trying to get rid of me already? We haven't even gone to California yet."

She clarified her question. "I was just wondering how long you'd be here once we get back from the trip."

"I've got a clinic scheduled in Wyoming, but it's only for a weekend. I could drive there from here, then come back afterward, if I keep the cabin a little longer. After that, I'll be going to New Mexico to meet with a new client."

"So that's when you'd be leaving for good?"

He bit into the sandwich. "Not for good, Bridget. I'd be coming back at some point to see Cody again."

"I know. That wasn't what I was implying." She changed the subject, switching back to California. "Why don't you tell me more about Tanner and his fiancée, so I know what to expect?"

"Tell you what about them, exactly?"

"For starters, what type of house do they have? Will we be staying at their place or renting rooms? Oh, and what's her name? You've hardly said anything about her."

"Her name is Candy. She and Tanner used to date when they were teenagers, but they broke up soon after Ella died. Tanner took our sister's death and our parents' divorce really hard, and he couldn't handle the pressure of having a girlfriend, too."

"But now they're engaged, all these years later? How did that happen?"

"They got reacquainted when a mutual friend put them back in touch. Candy was selling her house just at the time Tanner was looking to buy one. He needed a place that had a guesthouse so he could provide accommodations for Meagan when she gets out of prison."

"Did Tanner buy Candy's house?"

"Yes, he did. And now they live there together with Meagan's baby. I haven't seen his property yet, but Tanner told me that he remodeled the guesthouse and made it bigger, so it'll suit Meagan and her daughter later on." Kade swigged his water. "That's where you and Cody and I will be staying. It's only two bedrooms, but I can crash on the couch."

She wasn't keen on sleeping in the same house with Kade. Nor did she want to stumble upon him every morning. Better to have him behind a closed door. "Cody can stay on the couch. He doesn't need his own room while we're on vacation."

"That's fine. It doesn't matter to me."

Bridget didn't have much control over the situation, but at least she'd gotten the sleeping arrangements settled.

"Tanner has an apartment above the office at his stables, too," Kade said. "That's where he used to live before he bought Candy's house. He plans on renting it out since he doesn't need it anymore. It's a bachelor pad. My brother used to play around a lot."

Yet he was settling down to get married. That made Bridget more interested in the woman who'd tamed him. "What does Candy do for a living?"

"When she was younger, she was a beauty queen.

Then she got into modeling. But these days, she teaches yoga."

Tanner's fiancée sounded beautiful and trendy and everything California girls were supposed to be. "What's her personality like?"

"I only met her once, and that's when she and Tanner were teenagers. It was when I came home for Ella's funeral, so it wasn't a good time for any of us. But from what I recall, she was a really nice girl. She was crazy about my brother, even back then."

"Is she the tall blond surfer type?"

"When I saw her, she was a long, lean brunette. So unless she changed her hair color or has gotten curvier since then, I suspect she looks the same. Only more grown up, I guess."

"So you haven't seen any recent pictures?"

"Of Candy? No. But since Tanner has been sending pictures of Ivy, I'm getting accustomed to seeing the baby. He says she's a really happy kid, and that's what matters."

Bridget nodded. Kade was right. It was the children who mattered. She'd agreed to take this trip only because of how important it was to Cody. "Do you have any pictures of Ivy on you?"

"Sure." He removed his phone from his pocket and scrolled his finger along the screen, going through his text messages. "Here you go. Tanner sent it last week, so it's the most current one I have."

She took the device and looked at the image. "Oh, my goodness. How adorable is she?" The picture showed a baby with big brown eyes, chipmunk cheeks, a winning smile and fluffy dark hair. "I like the headband bow she's wearing. And her frilly little outfit. I wish I could've had a girl, too."

Kade got a startled expression. "How would that have worked? With us having twins?"

Yikes. She hadn't meant to say it quite like that. "I didn't mean having two babies with you, Kade."

He frowned. "Then, how did you mean it?"

"I was just saying that if I'd gotten married and had another child, I would've liked having a girl." She thought about her current situation. "I never expected to have a baby out of wedlock. I don't regret it because I love Cody so much. But I'm really careful now about using birth control." She couldn't handle another un-planned pregnancy. "I'm on the Pill even though I hardly ever date or sleep with anyone."

He kept frowning. "There's still time for you to get married and have more kids."

She returned his phone. "Yes, but I'd have to meet the right man and fall in love and do all of that com-plicated stuff." She didn't see how it was possible, not with how picky she was about the men she dated. But being alone for the rest of her life would be terribly painful. She couldn't fathom that, either. "I try not to think about it too much."

"I don't know anything about being in love. But Tan-ner was a mess when he was falling for Candy."

Curious to know more, she asked, "When they were teenagers or recently?"

"Recently. Right before they got engaged."

"How do you know he was a mess?"

Kade reached for a leaf that drifted onto the blan-ket. "He called me when it was happening. He'd been up all night, freaking out about his feelings for her, and he needed someone to talk to."

She hadn't expected to be so fascinated by his relationship with his brother. "So you helped him through it?"

"Given the circumstances, I did the best I could. He was scared beyond belief and trying to figure out if he loved her. I told him that he needed to work that out himself. But I also told him not to drag his feet, or else he might lose her."

Now Bridget was even more fascinated. She wouldn't have foreseen Kade giving that sort of advice. "I'm impressed."

"With me? Don't be. Tanner used to get scared when we were kids, too. He'd watch a creepy movie and want me to talk him out of being afraid."

"Being afraid of a creepy movie isn't the same as the fear of falling in love."

Kade shrugged. "Maybe it is. I mean, how the heck would we know?"

"We wouldn't." But nonetheless, she was having scary thoughts of her own, the urge to kiss him floating in and out of her head. To combat the feeling, she sat up and drew her knees to her chest.

He tossed the leaf aside. "If our dad hadn't screwed with our heads when we were young, my brother probably would have become a family man a long time ago."

She wrapped her arms around her knees. "But not you?"

"No, not me. I've always needed to be free, even if I never played around the way Tanner did."

Bridget tightened her grip, wishing the urge to kiss

him would go away. "No one is taking your freedom away from you."

"I didn't say anyone was." He gazed softly at her. "I like being Cody's dad. This thing with you and me is tough, though, but we're getting through it."

"Are we, Kade?"

"We're trying," he said, in a voice that indicated his struggle. "We both agreed that nothing was going to happen."

True to their word, neither of them caved in. They finished their picnic and rode back to her house, without the slightest touch between them.

The California trip was getting closer, and by now Cody had finished his comic. Kade wasn't faring quite so well, at least not with his personal contribution to the time capsule. He hadn't written the note yet. He was working on it today, but the sentences just wouldn't come.

He was at Bridget's house, sitting at her kitchen table. She'd gone shopping with Maura in town. Cody and his ginger-haired friend Jason were in the living room, playing video games. They'd made a mess in there, with snacks and toys and all sorts of junk strewn about.

"It's time to clean up that mess," Kade called out to them, concerned that Bridget might be back sooner rather than later.

"We will," Cody told him, without budging from the couch.

Kade rolled his eyes. He wasn't going to nag his son. But dang if the kids didn't listen. "Don't blame me if your mom gets mad."

"She won't care. She'll be in a good mood after going shopping."

Somehow Kade didn't see that as being true. Bridget was fanatical about keeping the living room tidy.

The boys got louder, laughing and carrying on, but he tuned out their shenanigans, staring at the blank paper in front of him. He wasn't stuck on what to say about Cody. He knew he could easily write that part. It was Bridget who was giving him trouble. How should he define his relationship with her? What was he supposed to say about the mother of his child? Nothing came to mind, except for how badly he wanted her, and he couldn't say that.

The front door opened, and he cursed beneath his breath. Bridget was home with Maura in tow. He could hear both of their voices.

He got up, leaving the paper and pen on the table. He entered the living room and winced. Bridget and Maura stood there, staring at the chaos Cody and Jason had created.

Oh, what the hell. Kade grabbed his cell phone and snapped a picture of the boys, mired in their mess, to go along with the rest of the pictures he'd been taking for the time capsule.

Bridget gaped at him. "Seriously, that's your reaction to this?"

Maura laughed and said to him, "Remind me not to use you as my babysitter."

As if he would ever watch her kids. The one in the oven wasn't even fully cooked yet. "I told them to clean it up."

Maura laughed again. "Yes, and I can see how well they obey you."

Bridget wasn't amused. Nor did she let their son off the hook. "*Cody Colton Wells*. You've got five minutes to restore order or you're grounded."

The boy leaped to attention, with Jason springing up to help him. Kade didn't doubt it would be spic and span in less than the allotted time.

Maura rubbed salt in his wound. "See that, Daddy? See how quickly and efficiently Mommy got it done?"

Kade wanted to defend himself, explaining that Mommy had lots of practice, but he decided not to argue his case.

Instead, he steered the conversation in another direction. Noticing that she'd placed a package by the front door, he causally asked Bridget, "What did you buy?"

Her mood brightened; so Cody was right about that. She replied, "We went to a new baby boutique so Maura could check it out. Then I spotted some things I thought would be cute for Ivy."

"You bought my niece some gifts?"

"Yes, of course. I can't go there and not bring the baby anything. Do you want to see what I got?" She grabbed the bag and opened it. "Look at this romper. Isn't it darling?" She jiggled the Western-themed garment. "It even has booties to match."

"That is cute. I'm sure Tanner and Candy will love it."

"I got this, too." She reached into the bag and pulled out a little T-shirt with *Cowgirl in Training* stitched on the front of it.

"Another great find." He fingered the hem of the shirt. "My brother is eager to put Ivy up on a horse with him."

"I can add your name on the card if you want, and say the gifts are from all of us."

"No, that's okay. They can be just from you and Cody. I bought some savings bonds in her name when she was first born. I'm practical that way, I guess." Plus he didn't have a clue how to shop for babies.

"My kid is due at the end of August. In case you want to contribute," Maura said, teasing him.

He smiled, thinking he just might do that. "So what are you having this time? A boy or another girl?"

"A boy. Want an introduction?" She took Kade's hand and placed it on her belly. "Just wait for a second, and I guarantee that he'll kick you."

He decided not to feel weird about touching her stomach, not when she seemed so comfortable about it. And sure enough, the unborn tyke jabbed him. The sudden movement made Kade laugh.

Maura laughed, too. "My little football player."

"Most definitely." Kade removed his hand and noticed that Bridget was watching him. "Did Cody kick like that?" he asked.

She nodded and put the things she'd bought for Ivy back in the bag. She seemed reflective. Was she reminiscing about Cody when he was curled up in her womb? Or was she contemplating the future babies she didn't know if she was ever going to have?

Kade certainly couldn't offer to have another child with her. He wasn't a sperm donor. Nor was he capable of being a second-time dad. He was still learning how to parent the first one. Regardless, he didn't like thinking of Bridget having a kid with someone else.

"I better get going," Maura said. "My husband is

home alone with our daughter, and they've probably made a mess out of the house by now, too."

Bridget walked her friend out, and after she returned, Kade said, "I won't let Cody tear the place apart again."

"Thanks. I appreciate that. I'm going to get started on dinner. Do you want to stay and join us?"

"No, thanks." He needed to escape the things that were rambling around in his head. Seriously, why should it matter who fathered Bridget's next kid, as long as it wasn't him? "I'm going to relax at the cabin." And open a can of ravioli or chili or something. He didn't care what he ate. All he wanted was to hightail it out of there.

"What's this?" Bridget asked as she entered the kitchen.

Shoot, now he had to explain the empty note he'd left on the table. "It's what I'm working on for the time capsule."

"It's blank."

"I'm still figuring out what to write." He grabbed the paper and pen and shoved them in his pocket, as if he had something to hide. "I'm going to say goodbye to Cody and take off." Before his mind exploded from the beautiful confusion that was Bridget.

Bridget labored over the clothes on her bed, trying to decide what to bring on vacation. She hadn't seen much of Kade lately, and the trip was just a few days away. Mostly he'd been entertaining Cody and his friends. Just yesterday, he'd taken a passel of kids fishing, and afterward, he and Cody had camped out in his back-yard. Their son was having the time of his life, and he was still in Montana. She could only imagine how much fun he was going to have when they got to California.

She wasn't offended that Kade was avoiding her. She needed to distance herself from him, too. But with the trip just around the bend, they were going to have to fall back into the pattern of being around each other again.

The doorbell rang, and Bridget went to answer it, wondering if the person on the other side was Kade. No, that didn't make sense. Cody and Kade were together today, and Cody wouldn't have used the bell.

She flung open the door and saw her grandmother. The older woman stood on the porch, her long silver hair catching the setting rays of the sun.

"I brought this for Cody," Grandma said, extending a canvas bag. "It's the items he chose to represent Grandpa in the time capsule. I thought you could pack them for him."

"Of course. Do you want to come in?"

"Yes, thank you." Grandma entered the house.

Bridget looked in the bag and saw a picture of Grandpa when he was in the navy. His dog tags were in there, too, along with the Santa hat he always wore at Christmas. Her heart went tight. "You don't mind parting with all of this?"

"Goodness, no. I think it's an honor."

"Then, I'll pack them, for sure." Bridget sighed. "I was just going through my clothes, trying to figure out what I should bring for the trip."

"Need some help?"

"That would be great."

She brought Grandma to her room, and they sat on opposite sides of the bed.

"This is cute." The older woman lifted a blue gingham sundress from a stack that hadn't been sorted yet. "You can wear it with sandals or boots."

"You don't think it will make me look like I'm headed to a barn dance?"

"No, sweetie. It flatters you. These khaki shorts will work, too. Oh, and this little number." Her grandmother pointed out a short-sleeved blouse with a round collar. "The white eyelet is pretty."

"Thanks." She placed her grandmother's selections in the "maybe" pile. "I'm so nervous about going that I can't think straight."

"I know. But it will be good for you to get away. To fly for the first time. To be somewhere other than your hometown."

"If you say so." Bridget eyed a long brown skirt, debating on whether to accept or reject it.

"What's happening with the prison situation?"

"You mean with the visitation? Cody and I were approved. We're on the list to see Meagan."

"I already told Kade that I think it will be good for Cody to have that experience with him. I think it will bring them closer together."

"I'm trying to be careful not to get too close to Kade."

"I'm well aware of that. It's a different kind of closeness you two are fighting, though. It's beyond me why you don't just give in to it."

Goodness, gracious. "Grandma, *really.*"

"Really what? Life is short. If you don't grab it by the horns, it'll be gone before you know it."

"I'd rather not take any chances."

"Of what? Getting hurt? Immersing yourself in fear is foolish."

Bridget shook her head. "Mom would be giving me advice to watch my step."

"You and your mother are too cautious."

"If I throw caution to the wind and it makes things worse, then Mom and I would have been right."

"And if you keep yourself cooped up in an emotional corner, you'll never know how exciting taking chances can be."

"I already took a chance when I was with Kade the first time."

"And you got a wonderful child as a result of it."

"I know, and I'm grateful that I have Cody." He was everything to her. "But I'm older and wiser now, and I have to be more careful. If Kade hurts me again, I'll never get over it."

"That's not a healthy way to think. But I'll stop pestering you about it. Just do what feels right, and you'll be okay."

Meaning what? If kissing Kade felt right, then she should go ahead and indulge? "You're a bad influence on me."

Her grandmother laughed. "I certainly try. But I'm not the only one who nudges you into having a little fun. Maura does that, too."

Yes, Maura with her cozy married life. "She's always been more daring than I could ever be." Yet her friend had everything Bridget dreamed of having. "Maybe I really should take more chances."

"That's my girl." Grandma flashed a chipper smile. "And don't worry about anything while you're gone. I'll take care of your job, your house and your horses."

"Thank you." She paused to collect her thoughts. "Do you want to see the toy necklace I'm going to put in the time capsule?" She went to her closet and re-moved it from the box where she kept it. "Kade gave it to me from before." She explained the story behind it, recounting the details.

Grandma opened the egg-shaped container and ex-amined the necklace, the gold tin hearts and shiny paste stones winking in the lamplight. "It's a lovely little thing. I don't remember the one you had as a child. But I can envision you wearing it."

"I wouldn't dare try to put that one on. It's too small for an adult. It's not very sturdy, either. I'd probably break it like I did the original one." And she couldn't bear to shatter the sentiment.

"What is Kade going to put in the capsule?"

"He's been taking a bunch of pictures for it. But he's also writing a note about Cody and me. I have no idea if he's composed it yet. The last time I saw any evidence of it, the page was blank."

"He probably just wants to make the words count."

"He's going to keep it sealed. But I wish he would let me read it." Her interest hadn't waned. If anything, it had gotten stronger.

"Maybe he'll change his mind when the time comes and show it to you."

"I suppose I could ask him how it's going or if he finished it."

Grandma tucked the necklace back into its egg and returned it to her. "This is a nice token from the past."

That Bridget had chosen to bury for the duration of its existence. She pressed the container to her chest, re-membering when it had rolled out of the gumball ma-chine and into Kade's hand. In the recesses of her mind, it seemed like a lifetime ago. Yet the rush of emotion felt fresh and new.

Her grandmother resumed sorting through the clothing for Bridget's trip. "Just do your best to enjoy your vacation and have as much fun as you can."

"I'll try." Bridget lowered the necklace Kade had given her, suddenly aware that she'd been holding it much too close to her heart.

Chapter Nine

Kade, Bridget and Cody were midway to California. They'd already changed planes in Denver, and now they were on the last leg of their flight.

Kade glanced over at Bridget to see how she was faring. She seemed calm enough. She even smiled at him.

"So do you like flying?" he asked.

"It's getting easier. Except for the takeoffs and landings. Those still make me a little nervous. But otherwise, I can't even tell that we're moving."

So far there hadn't been any turbulence, so they hadn't gotten bumped around. "Cody is enjoying it."

"No kidding. Look at him."

They both glanced over at their son. With earbuds planted firmly in his ears, he was munching on pretzels, drinking orange juice and watching a TV show he'd selected. Their newly refurbished plane was equipped with in-flight entertainment, located in seatback screens in front of each first-class passenger.

"Do you know what he told me earlier?" Bridget asked. "That when he grows up, he wants be a pilot."

"Did he just decide that today?"

She nodded. "I always envisioned him running the farm equipment business someday. Not that it's up to me to decide. But it's just what everyone in my family has done."

"The pilot thing will probably pass. Kids always change their minds about what they want to do."

"I know. But it's strange to see him becoming so cosmopolitan."

Kade chuckled. "Is that what he's doing?"

"That's how it seems to me." She laughed a little, too. "Well, maybe not with the way he's cramming those pretzels into his mouth, but you get the idea."

"Yeah, I do." Kade studied her, thinking how pretty she looked, with her hair neatly braided and her Western-style blouse tied at the waist. A country girl on the way to the city. "What did you want to be when you were a kid? Did you ever have any aspirations beyond working for your family's business?"

"When I was really little I wanted to be a princess. I didn't have a clue how I was going to do that, though. Other than to marry a prince."

"That's what Grace Kelly did."

"Is she another of your favorite pinup actresses?"

"She wasn't known for being a pinup, per se, but she was known for her elegance and beauty. I read that she was actually quite wild. But somehow she got past it without her public persona being tarnished. Some reports even say that she tricked her groom into thinking that she was still a virgin when she'd already bedded most of her leading men. I don't know if there's any truth to that. Whatever the case, she was considered the ultimate in class and breeding."

"Then, it makes sense that she married a prince." Bridget sighed like a schoolgirl. "I'll bet their wedding was really grand. Like those old clips of Charles and Diana. And William and Kate, of course. I watched every moment of theirs."

"I didn't pay much attention to it." Kade didn't want to discuss marriage, royal or otherwise. But he did want to undo the plaits in Bridget's hair and run his fingers through each silky strand.

"So what did you want to be?" she asked.

He'd zoned out. "What?"

"When you were a kid."

Oh, right. The career-options conversation. He forced his mind to focus. "I don't remember the very first thing I ever thought about doing. It might have been flying around in a cape and saving the world."

"As a superhero? Well, what do you know? That's what you've become. In our son's comic book."

"Then, I guess he had me pegged right from the start." Except Cody had put a superhero mom and a ten-year-old kid by his side. Kade wouldn't have imagined that part. Even now, it seemed surreal, traveling with this woman and their child.

She reached for the coffee she'd been drinking. "What do you remember wanting to be? What was your first conscious choice?"

He sipped his coffee, too. "A cowboy."

"And that's just what you are."

"Technically, I'm a horse trainer."

"To me, that still makes you a cowboy. When I look at you, that's what I see."

And she was looking at him—intently—directly over the rim of their cups. He put his down before he spilled it.

"What's wrong?" she asked. "Isn't it sweet enough?"

It was plenty sweet: the coffee and her. She was starting to seem like a princess. Or a bride. Or something he had no business wanting. "It's fine. I just don't feel like finishing it."

"I need the buzz from mine. I'm already noticing the time change."

"There's only an hour difference, and we aren't even there yet."

"I know. But I didn't sleep very well last night, so I'm feeling that, too."

Before he could stop his mind from betraying him, he pictured her in bed, dressed in her wholesome pajamas. Unfortunately, it wasn't any safer than recalling how she looked when she was naked. He found either image enticing. "Hopefully you'll sleep better tonight."

"I'm going to try. But I want to be awake when we get there. I'm interested in getting to know your family."

"They're interested in knowing you, too."

She kept her hands wrapped around her cup. "I've been wondering about something."

"What?"

"If you completed the note for the time capsule."

"Not yet." He was still stuck on what to say about Bridget. Every time he wrote something about her, it sounded too romantic and he tossed it out and started over, only to come up with more of the same. "But I'll get it done."

"When does Tanner plan on having the ceremony?"

"He scheduled it for later in the week. I'll have to go through the storage unit and get something of Mom's and Ella's to put in."

"You're not concerned about having to hurry?"

"It won't take long to go through the boxes. Everything is labeled and organized. I might even do it today, if there's time. The storage facility is just down the street from where Tanner lives."

"I was talking about finishing the note."

He faked a casual response. "It's no big deal. I work better under pressure. Besides, the note was my idea. No one is putting me up to it."

"Just for the record, I'd love to read it. I can't help being curious."

He made a stupid joke. "Maybe you better stop being so curious. They say that's what killed the cat, you know."

She rolled her eyes. "Never mind, smarty. I can do without your wisecracks. Or your creative writing skills, if you even have any talent in that department. The part about me will probably be boring anyway."

Was she trying to use reverse psychology on him? If so, it wasn't working. Whatever words he used to describe her would be far from dull. "Nice try, but I'm not falling for that."

She made puppy eyes at him. "What if I beg? Would that sway you?"

As cute as she looked, this new tactic of hers wasn't effective, either. He wasn't going to let her read the dang thing, no matter what antics she pulled. "No dice, Bridget. I'm not giving in."

"Fine. Be that way." Ending their discussion, she

plugged into the screen in front of her and scanned the entertainment that was available.

Kade didn't bother with his. Once the plane landed and they drove to his brother's place, there was going to be plenty of noise. For now, he preferred to slip into silence and watch the clouds floating by.

As everyone gathered in the backyard, drinking lemonade and socializing, Bridget couldn't help but analyze the people who were there.

Tanner was wildly handsome, with short dark hair, deep-set eyes and a chiseled jaw. He looked a lot like Kade. He had a similar sense of humor, too. There was no mistaking that they were brothers.

As for Candy, she was kind and genuine and easily likable. She was also the most gorgeous woman Bridget had ever seen. It was tough not to gawk at her. She stood tall and trim, with straight chestnut-colored hair and elegant features. She wore a simple outfit—an oversize T-shirt and leggings—but it could have been a ball gown from the graceful way she carried herself.

And the baby! Ivy was an adorable creature, dressed in ruffles and bows. She clung to Tanner, bubbling over in his arms.

Then there was the dog.

Candy owned a yellow Lab named Yogi who was warm and friendly and incredibly well behaved. Cody sat on the grass beside her, ruffling her fur.

"This is a beautiful garden," Bridget said to Candy. Color burst from flower beds and vines grew in tangled beauty, creeping along trellises. Carefully cultivated fruit trees, from which the lemonade had been made, scented the summer air.

"Thank you," Candy replied. "I designed it long before Tanner bought the house. But now he loves it, too. We spend a lot of time out here." She gestured across the yard. "I hope you enjoy the garden that's attached to the guesthouse."

"I'm sure we will." Bridget glanced toward the place where she, Cody and Kade would be staying. With its whimsical style, it looked like something out of a storybook. It even had a fountain out front. The interior was lovely, too. They'd already been given a quick tour and put their bags away. She tried not to think about what spending the next two weeks there was going to feel like, though, with Kade sleeping under the same gingerbread roof.

Bridget shifted her gaze to Kade. For the time being, he was rather quiet, mostly just listening to the conversation, rather than joining in.

Cody said, "Yogi is the coolest dog. I wish I could have one just like her."

Candy smiled. "She works with me at the yoga studio. I teach doga along with yoga. Doga is a bonding experience pet owners can have with their dogs. It's done through meditation, stretching and gentle massage." She went over to Cody and Yogi. "Here, we'll demonstrate." She got into a bendy pose, leaning forward on the ground, and the dog hopped up to emulate her.

Bridget thought it was just the sweetest thing. Naturally Cody did, too. He grinned from ear to ear. Ivy reacted as well, letting out a squeal and a clap.

Tanner chuckled. "Ivy always applauds Yogi when she exercises with Candy. But not all dogs are as talented as Yogi. Some of the poses only require dogs to relax while their owners rub their bellies. But that's still part of the experience."

Candy resumed an upright position and said to Cody, "I can teach you some of the poses and you can do them with Yogi."

"Okay. Wow. That'll be fun." He was still grinning. "I love California already." He was beside himself with vacation joy, and it was only the first day.

"Is anyone hungry?" Tanner asked. "We can order pizza."

"Definitely," Cody responded, always eager to eat.

Pepperoni was the topping preferred by everyone except Candy. She was a vegetarian, so she opted for mushrooms, onions and bell peppers.

While Tanner called in the order, Candy took charge of Ivy, holding her close and rocking her back and forth.

"I used to be her nanny," she told Bridget. "That was before Tanner asked me to marry him."

"Really?" Bridget wouldn't have pictured her as the hired help. "How did that come about?"

"After he bought my house and moved in, the nanny he'd arranged for had a family emergency on the same day that Ivy was born, and he didn't have anyone to help him. So he panicked and asked me."

Tanner hung up the phone and joined the conversation. "It was the best decision I ever made," he said. "Candy was just what Ivy and I needed. Marrying her is going to be everything it should be."

Without a doubt, they were a happily engaged couple living out their dream. "When do you plan to set the date?" Bridget asked.

"We haven't decided," Candy answered. "We actually might wait a few years so Meagan can be part of the wedding. We take Ivy to see her mama as often as we can."

Tanner frowned. "Meagan went through a really rough patch soon after Ivy was born and wanted us to adopt her. But we think that was coming from a place of depression, not because she wanted to let her daughter go."

Candy added, "So we're just seeing how things unfold. If Meagan still wants us to be Ivy's parents later on, we would love to adopt her. If not, then Ivy will always be our niece, and Meagan and her daughter will always be welcome to live here."

Tanner softened his expression. "Either way, Candy and I are going to have more kids. There are going to be lots of little Quinns running around."

Bridget couldn't imagine two people who were more suited to parenthood. "That's nice to hear."

Tanner smiled. "Thanks."

"I knew Meagan was sad," Kade said, coming out of his quiet mood to comment on his sister. "But I didn't know that she'd talked to you about adopting Ivy."

His brother replied, "I didn't tell you when the discussion first came up because there was so much else going on then. But now that Candy and I are settled, we're better equipped to help Meagan through her depression."

"Is she improving?" Kade asked.

"Yes, she definitely is. She still has her moments, but overall she's been making great strides. She loves seeing Ivy. And she's happy that you'll be visiting her. She's excited about getting to know your son, too. It's great to have him as part of this brood." Tanner turned to Bridget. "You raised a great kid."

"Thank you." She was proud of her boy and pleased that he was fitting in so well. "That's really nice to hear."

Thirty minutes later the pizza arrived, and the weather was so beautiful that they decided to eat in the backyard. Candy fixed food for Ivy, too, and moved her high chair outside.

After the meal, Kade mentioned that he was going to head over to the storage facility before the sun went down. He invited Cody to accompany him, but the dog-smitten ten-year-old wanted to stay and play with Yogi.

Kade looked at Bridget. "How would you like to come with me?"

"Sure. Why not?" She was interested in seeing what he was going to choose for the time capsule.

Normally, as an overprotective mom, she wouldn't have left Cody by himself in a new environment. But he was perfectly content where he was, not just with the dog, but with his father's family, too.

Everywhere Kade looked, there were cartons and crates and boxes that represented pain from the past. But he wasn't doing this to stir up bad memories. He had a positive agenda.

He located three boxes that were marked "Photos" and set them aside. "I'll take these back to the house and go through them there. I'm sure there's a picture of Mom with Ella that I can use. But I need to find some other mementos, like the things your grandmother provided of your grandfather's."

"You were right about this place being organized." Bridget glanced around. "Who stored everything this way? So neatly labeled and stacked?"

"Meagan. She had a tough time parting with anything that belonged to Mom, so she boxed up as much of it as she could. We can't keep all this forever, though. But Tanner would never get rid of any of it without talking to Meagan first. And I doubt she's ready to deal with it, not when she has so many other things on her mind. I'm relieved that she's getting better, though. I couldn't have handled seeing her when she was at her most depressed."

"I'm glad she's excited about seeing you and Cody. I'm curious to meet her, too. I can't imagine her wanting to give up her baby for adoption. But if she does make that choice, I can see why she would choose Tanner and Candy as Ivy's parents. It's obvious how much they love her."

"I love *our* son, too, Bridget." He looked into her eyes, needing her to know that he meant it.

She returned his gaze, her breath catching, her voice cracking. "It's good to hear you say those words about him."

"I haven't said them to him yet, and he hasn't said them to me, either. I guess we will when the moment feels right."

Still gazing directly at him, she nodded in agreement. "I'm sure you will."

"My dad never said that to me or to any of us kids. He never said anything warm and kind. Our mom did. But sometimes she overdid it, though. She coddled us to make up for how cold and indifferent he was."

"There was no balance in your lives?"

"No, there was none. We didn't understand what being a family meant. We tried, but it all just seemed so messed up, especially after Ella died. I went back to school to escape, but Tanner got stuck with everything that came after it. Candy tried to help him through it, but he rejected her back then."

"They're a really happy couple now."

"They sure seem to be." But that wasn't the case with most couples. Was it?

Kade honestly didn't know. Nor did he want to ponder the subject too deeply. He didn't need to crowd his mind with other people's lives, not when his own was changing at such a rapid pace. Not only had his feelings for Cody become deeply ingrained, but his attraction to Bridget kept getting stronger, and that wasn't supposed to be part of the deal.

He reached for a box that was marked "Mom's jewelry." He knew it wasn't going to be gold or diamonds. She'd worn only the fake stuff, but maybe he would uncover something that he could put in the time capsule.

"Will you go through this with me?" he asked Bridget.

"Yes, of course. I'd be glad to help."

He opened the hatchback of the SUV he'd rented, and they sat on the tailgate. The contents of the box turned out to be a bit of a mess, beads and baubles twined together.

"Your mom had lots of bling," Bridget said as they worked to separate it. "Do you remember any pieces that were particularly special to her?"

"No. But she always looked really pretty when she went out. She enjoyed wearing fancy things, but she was still a country girl at heart."

Bridget clutched two strands of tangled pearls. "I think I would have liked her."

"I think she would have liked you, too." He was still

itching to undo Bridget's proper little braid, to touch her hair, to feel the softness. "You're the type of girl she would have wanted me to date. Or marry, or whatever, if I was that sort of guy. But she accepted me for who I was."

She glanced up. "A loner?"

He nodded, and they both fell silent. He shouldn't have mentioned the marriage part. He wasn't sure what had compelled him to say it, other than maybe his brother's picture-perfect engagement.

Trying to ease the tension, he said, "Mom would certainly be glad how things turned out for Tanner. She would be happy to know I have a son, too. She would've never expected that of me."

"You didn't expect it, either."

"No, but now I can't imagine not being a dad."

Bridget smiled, and they continued their task. But by the time they got through it, Kade still didn't know what to use.

"None of this is going to work," he said.

"You can't force it."

"I know. But I thought it would be easier. That something would magically appear, I guess." He closed the box and resealed the tape. "Maybe I thought I was going to find a necklace like yours."

"My necklace came out of a gumball machine. What's the likelihood that your mom would've have had an item like that?"

"I meant with the same kind of sentiment attached. I can't just put something in the time capsule that has no meaning. Or that I don't feel anything for."

"You just need to keep trying."

"But what if nothing feels right?" What would that say about him and how disconnected he was?

"Don't give up." She gestured to the storage unit. "There's something in there waiting for you to find it. All you have to do is look."

"Okay." Appreciating her encouragement, he left her sitting on the tailgate and returned to the building.

Four boxes later, he uncovered a Christmas ornament with a silver-winged fairy on it, and he knew Bridget was right. That all he'd had to do was look.

He brought it over and held it out to her. Specs of glitter dusted his hand. "Mom put this on the tree every year after Ella died." He would never forget how significant it was.

"That will work for both of them, Kade."

"I think so, too. But do you know why Mom bought it in the first place? The name Ella means 'beautiful fairy.'"

"Oh, my." Bridget took the ornament and held it toward the waning sunlight. "Ella isn't just an angel. She's a fairy."

He nodded, missing his mom and baby sister, but glad that Bridget was here, sharing such a special moment with him.

As night approached, darkening a set of etched-glass windows in the living room of the main house, Bridget glanced over at Kade. They sat side by side on the sofa, with Tanner and Candy seated across from them. Cody was there, too, on the floor with the dog. Ivy was nearby as well, babbling in her playpen.

The adults were sorting through the boxes of photographs Kade had brought back from the storage unit.

It was a group effort, and Bridget felt very much a part of it. In fact, she was feeling closer to Kade than she'd ever been.

She was even tempted to put her hand on his knee. But she didn't touch him. She noticed that Candy was resting her hand on Tanner, though. But they were a couple, and she and Kade weren't. She wasn't in the position to take those sorts of liberties.

"Check this out," Tanner said.

He handed a photograph to Kade, and Bridget leaned over to see it. The image depicted two young boys dressed in matching shirts and posing with a palomino.

"Is that Brandy?" she asked, recalling the horse he'd told her and Cody about, the one he'd drawn the picture of when he was a kid.

"Yes, that's her. And Tanner and me in our Western finest. What the hell was Mom thinking, buying us the same shirt?"

"It wasn't Mom's fault," Tanner said. "I wanted to dress like you. I thought it made me look older."

"Yeah, well, all it did was make both of us look like dorks."

Tanner shrugged. "Speak for yourself. At least I wasn't grinning like a hyena."

Kade rolled his eyes, and Bridget reexamined the photo. Sure enough, the older boy was smiling like the dickens. Even then, Kade had the Dudley Do-Right thing down.

"Can I see it?" Cody asked.

"Here you go." Kade passed the picture to their son.

Cody studied it for a while. "Can we scan it so I can have a copy?"

"What for?" his uncle asked. "So you can blackmail your dad with it?"

"Ha. Ha." Kade pressed his thumb to his nose and wiggled his fingers at his brother.

Cody laughed at the way the men were behaving. They laughed at themselves, too. But when Kade uncovered an important photo, he stopped goofing around.

"This was taken right after Mom had Ella," he said. "I think it might've even been the day they came home from the hospital."

Bridget looked at the picture. Kade's mother had thick black hair and wide-set eyes, framed with luxurious lashes. She sat in a bentwood rocking chair, cradling her newborn daughter, whose tiny face peeked out from behind a white blanket.

"Your mom was lovely," she told him. "They both were."

"I knew her," Candy said. "And she was the nicest lady." She reached for Tanner's hand. "I knew Ella, too. And she was just the sweetest girl. Like our Ivy."

At the mention of her name, the baby grinned around the teething ring in her mouth. Bridget's heart all but melted.

"Can I hold Ivy?" she asked Candy.

"Oh, of course. She loves the attention."

Bridget got up and went over to the playpen. She knelt and spoke softly to the child. "Hello, darling. Do you want to come to me?"

Ivy dropped the teething ring and reached out to her new "aunt." Bridget scooped up the child and returned to the sofa. Ivy sat contentedly on her lap.

Kade dug through another box and discovered a photo album at the bottom of it. As he looked through it, Ivy tilted her head, watching him with interest. Obviously aware of her curious young eyes on him, he gazed up from a plastic-covered page to smile at her.

Now Bridget realized, *truly realized*, what she'd deprived him of by keeping Cody a secret. She'd taken his flesh and blood away from him, keeping Cody all to herself. But it was different now. Kade was part of their son's life.

Would he keep his promise to always be there? At the moment, she couldn't imagine him abandoning Cody, and she was grateful that her feelings about him were starting to change.

Kade turned another page and said to Tanner, "Look at this. It's you and Candy when you were teenagers."

"Oh, man. Let me see." His brother grabbed the album with boyish gusto. "I've thought a lot about this picture. It was taken at my junior prom." He leaned toward Candy, letting her view the photo, too. "How hot were you, in that sexy red dress that drove me wild? If I had any sense, I would've proposed to you back then."

She laughed and kissed him squarely on the mouth. Ivy clapped, the way she'd done when she'd applauded the dog. But she also puckered her lips, indicating that she was hankering for the same kind of kiss.

Kade quickly obliged. He lifted his niece from Bridget's lap and gave the little girl the sweetest, gentlest peck. Afterward, the baby snuggled against him, treating him like her hero.

Making him Bridget's latest, greatest hero, too.

Chapter Ten

As the days progressed, so did the activities. So far, Kade had taken Bridget and Cody to Disneyland, Universal Studios and Venice Beach. They hadn't hit the Walk of Fame yet, but that was on the agenda, along with whatever else they chose to do.

Another thing still on the list was visiting Meagan, but that would come later. It was easier for him to wait until the end of the trip to deal with everything that entailed, including the emotional impact of seeing his sister behind bars.

His immediate concern was finishing the note for the time capsule. The ceremony was tomorrow afternoon, and here it was, the night before, and he was scrambling to get it done.

He'd completed the parts about Cody. He knew just what to say about his son and their newfound relationship. But he kept hitting a wall every time he attempted to write about Bridget.

So maybe he should just leave her out of it. No, he thought. He couldn't do that. She was the woman who'd given birth to his child, the woman who consumed his thoughts. If he excluded her, the note would be incomplete.

For now, he sat alone in his room in the guesthouse, trying his damnedest to write about her. Finally, he just went for it. He jotted down whatever came to mind, even if it sounded romantic.

He chronicled the past: the horse training clinic where he and Bridget had met and the warm-hearted week they'd spent at the motel. He detailed every memory that mattered, including the mornings they'd eaten at the diner and their trip to the discount store where they'd gotten the toy necklace. He referenced the present, too: how they'd become reacquainted, why she hadn't told him about Cody to begin with and how important it was for Kade to prove himself to her now that he knew the truth…and, yeah, how badly he wanted her.

He folded the note, intending to slip it into an envelope and seal it. But then he got an impulse to show it to Bridget. In some oddly emotional way, he wanted her to know precisely what he'd written. And since she'd already pestered him about reading it, what harm was there in letting her take a look? He didn't see the point in keeping the note a mystery, at least not from her.

Instead of laboring over the decision, he walked into the hallway to see if she was still awake. She was, apparently, since a light glowed beneath her door.

He went farther down the hall to check on Cody. He was crashed out on the couch with the TV flickering on

Mute. On the floor beside him was a pile of souvenirs he'd collected, and the vacation wasn't even over yet. By the time they were ready to leave, they were going to have to buy an extra suitcase to bring his trove of treasures home.

Nonetheless, Kade smiled, pleased that his son was having such a good time.

Moving forward, he returned to Bridget's door. He knocked, and she appeared, wearing the wholesome pajamas he'd seen her in before. He hadn't gotten ready for bed yet, but for him that meant stripping down to the skin. He'd been sleeping in his underwear here, though, just so Cody didn't see him trailing to the bathroom bare-ass naked. He wouldn't have minded if Bridget caught a glimpse of his backside, but that was a whole other matter.

She gave him an uncertain look. "What's going on? Is something wrong?"

"No. I just wanted to let you read the time capsule note I wrote."

"Really?" She opened the door all the way. "Grandma said that you might change your mind and show it to me."

"When did she say that?"

"When I first told her about it."

Well, Grandma had been right. He had changed his mind. "May I come in?"

"Of course." She moved out of the way to allow him entrance.

Her room was decorated with furniture that had belonged to Candy, with brass accents and warmly textured woods. The furniture in Kade's room had come from Tanner's old bachelor apartment, reflecting a darker, bolder decor. Eventually some of it would be changed to accommodate Meagan and Ivy, depending on how that arrangement worked out.

Kade glanced at the bed. The sheets had already been turned down and the pillows looked freshly fluffed. He hoped that he was doing the right thing, showing up like a thief in the night. Being in such close proximity to where Bridget slept wasn't in his best interest.

She closed the door behind him, and the latch clicked into place. It was too late for him to rethink his decision, so he handed her the note.

She unfolded the paper, and while he stood there watching her, she read what he'd written.

Suddenly, he felt horribly exposed, as if his soul was dangling from his sleeve. Or bleeding from an open wound. He'd never put himself in a situation like this before, and it was painful as hell. With each thump of his heart, he studied her expression, hoping she would hurry up and get to the end.

When she finished, she looked up, and their gazes met and held. He could barely breathe, the air in his lungs refusing to cooperate.

"Well?" he asked, forcing himself to exhale. "Was it what you expected?"

"It was so much more, Kade. It was…" She couldn't seem to find the words. Until she said, "It was like the page out of a romantic journal. You covered everything beautifully."

"I kept struggling with it, but then I just gave up and wrote what came naturally."

She refolded the paper and returned it to him, her fingertips brushing his. "Thank you. That means a lot to me."

"You're welcome." Her touch, even as light as it was, sent shivers through his blood. "We should both get some sleep now. We have a big day tomorrow."

"Yes, we do." But the look on her face said that she didn't want him to leave. That she longed for him to stay in her room, to let the romance happen for real.

But could they be together, now, like this, with their son sleeping down the hall? He could tell those questions were also swirling around in her mind. Proper, cautious Bridget, struggling with her feelings, fighting reckless urges.

Kade fought them, too, waiting for her to decide. He wasn't going to try to sway her. As badly as he wanted her, the choice had to be hers. But she did nothing. Time merely ticked by, with uncertainty ringing in the air.

When he could no longer stand it, he said, "Do something, Bridget. Tell me to go. Or ask me to stay."

She hesitated, clutching the front of her pajama top, looking soft and pretty and nervous. Her breath rushed out before she said, "Stay."

His heart hammered in his chest. One word. One beautiful, anxious decision. Kade locked the door. Bridget was still holding on to her top, fingers tightly curled around the cotton fabric.

"Are you afraid?" he asked, moving toward her.

"Not of you," she replied. "Just of how I feel. I shouldn't want you this way. I should know better."

He gave her an out. "It's not too late to change your mind."

"I can't stop now. I just can't." She reached for him, pulling him close. "If it doesn't happen, the wanting will never go away. But if we do this…"

"You'll survive the feeling?" He leaned forward

to kiss her, the kiss they'd both been waiting for. He needed to survive it, too.

Their mouths came together in heat and fury, with passion that been building for far too long. Speed and desperation. That was all he could think, all he could feel.

He backed her against the bed, and they tumbled onto the mattress. All he wanted was to remove her chaste attire, to uncover her flesh, her warmth, the woman who wanted him as badly as he wanted her.

She tugged at his shirt, and they undressed each other, clothes flying off the side of the bed. But they were still quiet somehow, mindful of the child who slept down the hall.

This time, the risk of conceiving another baby was little to none. Bridget had already told him that she was taking birth control pills, even though she hardly ever dated.

Kade closed his hands over her, from breast to loin, devouring her nakedness, her luscious female curves. This wasn't a date, either. It was madness, sheer and simple.

"What are we doing?" she asked, clearly thinking the same thing.

He silenced her with a kiss, dark flashes of pleasure pulsing through his body. She raked her nails down his back, and he wasn't even inside her yet.

He tasted her in secret places, feasting on erotic flavors. She, in turn, stroked him until he thought he might die.

And then, only then, did they join forces, their bodies becoming one. They rolled over the bed with frantic gasps and possessive thrusts.

Buried to the hilt, he pounded into her. "This is going to happen fast."

"For me, too." Her ache was as violent as his. She clawed him even harder now, making catlike marks on his skin.

Kade didn't care. He liked this side her, the feline losing control.

Neither of them had thought to turn out the lights. An overhead lamp burned bright, giving him the opportunity to see exactly what he was doing to her.

He noticed that her hair was loose and messily strewn across the pillow, from where he'd tangled his hands in it.

Feeling big and strong and ruggedly male, he looked into the blueness of her eyes. He hoped that she didn't fall into regret when it was over. He knew that he wouldn't. But she was different from him. As throaty as her moans were, as aroused as she was, she still seemed vulnerable, fragile in a way that he couldn't deny. A part of him wanted to apologize, even if she was on the verge of orgasm.

This wasn't romance. This was sex. And somehow that didn't seem fair to her. But he couldn't change it now, even if he tried.

She closed her eyes when she came, shutting him out. He watched her, thinking how beautiful she was, her fair skin flushed with heat and color.

Kade watched until he could no longer see, until his vision blurred with the power of lust, with the woman convulsing beneath him. He spilled into her hard and fast, his blood roaring in his head.

Once it ended, she opened her eyes, both of them silent in the naked aftermath of what they'd just done.

* * *

Bridget's limbs went lax, her muscles quivering. Not only was her body in desperate need of recovery, so was her mind. Now that she'd let Kade ravish her, she was scared that she would never stop wanting him.

So what had she accomplished by sleeping with him if the wanting never went away? This was supposed to have helped her survive the feeling. But it hadn't.

He rolled off her, and she grabbed the sheet and covered herself with it, grappling for a semblance of modesty.

"I'm sorry," he said.

His apology made it worse, especially since he was reaching over the side of the bed for his clothes.

"It's okay," she told him. "I'm the one who invited you to stay."

"I know, but I should have made it gentler for you." He pulled on his underwear and climbed into his jeans. "I should have made it better."

Better? She was still reeling from his touch, from having had him inside her. Even the dampness from his seed was making her sensuously weak.

He sat next to her, with his chest bare, his muscles hard and ripped and gleaming with a light sheen of sexy sweat.

"Do you want to cuddle or anything?" he asked.

Heavens above. Could he complicate things any more than they already were? Now she was torn between curling up in his arms or bursting into postcoital tears.

She pulled the sheet closer to her body. "You don't have to feel responsible for me."

"I can't just leave you like this."

"I'm a big girl, Kade."

He ignored her claim. "I can sleep here if you want."

"No, you can't. I don't want Cody to figure out that we were together, and if he finds that you stayed the night in my room, I'd have to explain it somehow."

"Just tell him you had a nightmare and I came in to calm you down."

She shook her head. "I don't want to make up stories."

"But I'm already here, so what difference does it make?"

"I don't know." Maybe she was confused. Or maybe she just needed to relax. "I think I better get dressed." She removed her panties and pajamas from the floor.

As Kade watched her, she got dressed, then finger combed her hair, smoothing it the best she could.

He said, "You still look really pretty, even after the way I messed you up."

She went uncomfortably warm. He looked handsome, too, even with the scratches she'd left on his skin. "You need to put your shirt on."

"If I do, can I stay a little while?"

"Just put it on, Kade."

He pulled his T-shirt over his head. "I don't have to tuck it in, too, do I?"

"Was it tucked in when you first came into my room?"

"No."

"Then, it's fine." She glanced around, feeling far too scattered. But it was her own fault, her own choice to do what she'd done. "Where's the note you wrote?" The words that had been her undoing. That had urged her to be with him.

"I think I put it in my pocket." He checked his jeans. "It's here." He leaned forward, getting dangerously close to her. "I'm not going to pretend that this didn't happen. I'm going to make it more romantic next time."

"Next time?" She bit down on her bottom lip. It was already sore from how roughly they'd kissed.

"Yeah. Next time. Did you think I'd let you use me for one quick romp in the hay?"

She sputtered into laughter, the idea of her using him striking her as funny. Or impossible. Or something she couldn't quite name. "Who says I want it romantic?"

"Don't even try to convince me that you don't, because I won't believe you."

He was being rather aggressive for a man touting chivalry. He even pushed her down and kissed her, causing her lips to feel even more bruised.

He ended the kiss, and she cuddled in his arms, unable to resist him.

"You can only stay for a minute." Or two. Or three. "Then you have to go back to your own room."

"I will." He shifted his body so they could spoon.

Bridget loved the sensation of being warm and sweet, after having done something so wild. At least she wasn't fighting tears anymore. At least she was getting a grip on her emotions.

He stayed until she got sleepy. Then he skimmed her cheek and whispered, "I'm going to go now. Dream well, and I'll see you in the morning."

She closed her eyes and drifted off, missing him already.

Cody chatted up a storm over breakfast, and Bridget behaved as normally as she could, passing the salt and pepper shakers to Kade and trying not to look too closely at him.

Last night was starting to seem like a mirage, with images that didn't really exist. But she knew that wasn't the case. What had transpired between them had been real.

She picked at her food, moving the eggs and potatoes around on her plate. Finally, after Kade and Cody finished eating, she got up to do the dishes, grateful for the escape.

Kade got up, too, but returned to the table with his iPad computer tablet. He lingered over his second cup of coffee, burying his nose in the device. Cody headed into the living room to watch TV. But that didn't last. He got bored and went outside to play fetch with the dog.

Once he dashed out the door, Bridget breathed a little easier. She needed to converse with Kade, to get used to being around him again.

She casually asked, "What are you reading?"

He glanced up. "The website of a local paper. I wanted to see what was happening around here."

"Did you find anything interesting?"

"Actually, I did. Come here and I'll show you."

She moved closer, and he turned the screen toward her.

"It's a charity ball at a Beverly Hills hotel with an Old Hollywood theme. They're going to have cocktails by the pool, then dinner and dancing in an adjoining ballroom, with a live band that plays music from that era. They're also having a silent auction, where the attendees can bid on collector's items and old movie memorabilia. It's black tie, so it's pretty swanky."

She gazed at the screen. "It certainly looks as though they'll be pulling out all the stops."

"It's next Saturday, but there are still tickets left. Do you want to go?"

Her pulse jumped, from her stomach to her throat. "Are you inviting me on a date?"

"Yes, I am. I want to take you out on the town, and I think this would be the perfect place to go."

A big sparkling pool, a glitzy ballroom? Drinks, dinner, dancing? Her head swam with it. "Is this part of your plan to be romantic?"

He nodded. "Just think, Bridget. You and I in the moonlight, kissing under the stars, like people on dates are supposed to do." He searched her gaze, his dark eyes filled with concern. "Don't you want to go with me?"

Yes, God help her, she did. "It's just all happening so fast."

"Last night was fast," he countered. "But we won't rush this. I promise that you won't be disappointed."

Being disappointed was the least of her worries. He was making her swoon in ways she hadn't imagined. "It does sound intriguing."

"Then, let's do it. Let's make it happen."

"Okay, I'll go with you." She took a big breath, the kind she took when she was diving into the river at home. Only she wasn't home. She was on a vacation that was spiraling into a fancy ball. "But what should I do about a dress? You can rent a tux, but I'll have to buy something to wear." She didn't own a gown nor would she have thought to pack one, even if she did.

"You can ask Candy to take you shopping. We'll also have to ask her and Tanner if they can watch Cody. But I'm sure they won't mind." He let his gaze wander over her, up and down and all around. "I'll pay for your dress."

She shook her head, wishing he wasn't looking at her in that ravenous way of his. "You don't have to do that."

"I want to." He stopped checking her out and assumed a proper expression instead. "Besides, I offered to pay for everything on this trip, and I intend to keep my word."

"Thank you, then. I accept your offer." But she wouldn't overspend. What in the world was she going to do with a lavish gown later on, aside from cover it with plastic and hang it in her closet? Another thought quickly occurred to her. "I don't know how to dance to old music, to waltz or do any of the ballroom stuff. Do you?"

"No, but I can two-step pretty darned well."

Thankfully, she was accomplished at that, too. "So can I."

He smiled. "Then, we're halfway there. We'll just do what we know how to do and put our own spin on it."

"I'm looking forward to it, Kade." Nervous yet delighted, she smiled at him, too. This man who'd become her lover once again.

Chapter Eleven

Hours later, Bridget, Kade and Cody joined Tanner, Candy and Ivy at the stables Tanner owned.

Bridget thought it was a spectacular facility, with a big breezeway barn, indoor and outdoor arenas, round pens, wash racks and picnic areas. For the time capsule ceremony, Tanner had chosen a spot with a colorful view of the chaparral-lined trails that led to a nearby park.

The burial itself was simple, with Kade and his brother digging a four-foot-deep hole for the twin capsules. Both men said a few words about what an important occasion this was. They invited Cody to speak, too, and he chattered like the exuberant kid he was. Bridget chose to remain quiet, but Candy spoke up and said that she had something extra she planned to present.

Once the capsules were buried and the stone plaque

was in place, Candy removed pots of flowers and herbs from the back of Tanner's truck.

She explained that people in the Victorian era would communicate through the bouquets they exchanged, where each plant and flower had a specific meaning.

"It's called floriography," she said, "or the language of flowers."

Intrigued, Bridget asked, "How does that apply to this ceremony?"

Candy replied, "I thought we could create a garden surrounding the plaque, with a message that is unique to us. I chose sweet lavender because it means happiness and geraniums because they represent childhood. I did that for Cody and Ivy and Ella, since they are the children named on the plaque." She glanced at Tanner, who was holding Ivy gently in his arms. "The pink verbena signifies family union, so I figured that would be the main ingredient in this garden. Verbena is a spreading plant and will bloom all season. Oh, and I included lemon balm for love. Not just romantic love, but any kind of love."

Bridget couldn't imagine a nicer way to mark the occasion. "That's beautiful."

"Thank you." Candy provided gardening tools and gloves for each participant. "I'm glad you approve."

They worked as a team, planting the flowers and herbs. Cody was meticulous in his efforts, placing the geraniums just so. He also stopped Ivy from stuffing a palm full of compost into her mouth. But the baby, who was decked out in denim overalls and a floppy sunbonnet, wasn't deterred. She simply grabbed another handful and offered it to him instead.

Kade shot Bridget an amused look, and she returned

his smile. Cody wasn't having any luck making his cousin understand that he wasn't hungry for dirt, so he simply pretended to gobble it up. By now, Ivy had taken a shine to Cody, insisting on being near him. It made Bridget's heart glad to see how patient and loving he was with the baby. It also made her wish that she could give him a little brother or sister.

But that was a dangerous wish, especially while she and Kade were having an affair or a fling or whatever was happening between them. She didn't want to think about how it was going play out in the future. If she analyzed it too deeply or longed for more than Kade was capable of, the pain from the past was sure to repeat itself. But keeping her girlie feelings at bay wasn't easy, not with the romance he was determined to provide. The ball she'd agreed to attend was starting to seem like a fairy tale.

Before her thoughts ran away with her, she cleared her mind and returned her attention to the time capsule ceremony.

For the final touch, Tanner and Kade erected a border fence around the garden. Easily assembled, it was made of powder-coated steel, the gate decorated with an ornate design.

Bridget stood beside the others and gazed at the completed project, impressed and pleased with a job well done.

The gathering didn't end at the stables. It continued at the house with a late-day barbecue.

Bridget pitched in and helped Candy fix the food. They made salads and side dishes to go along with the steaks and veggie skewers that would be going on the grill.

While they were alone in the kitchen, Bridget asked, "Are you sure you won't mind keeping an eye on Cody on the night of the charity event?"

"No, of course not," Candy said. "It would be a pleasure to have him stay with us."

"I know Kade already talked to you and Tanner about it, but I just wanted to double-check."

"No worries. I'm looking forward to taking you shopping, too. Since you're concerned about the price, we could hit some secondhand stores and hunt for a vintage dress. My girlfriend did that for her wedding, and she found gorgeous gowns for herself and for the bridal party, too." Candy paused to clarify her comment. "Not that you're looking for wedding attire, but you know what I mean."

Yes, Bridget knew. She wasn't getting married, nor was she going to fantasize about walking down the aisle with Kade or anyone else. Still, she couldn't help but imagine how it would feel someday to be someone's wife.

Would she have her wedding near the river? In a church? In her grandma's backyard? Would it be formal? Or sweet and countrified? She could see it happening in all sorts of ways.

"So are you interested in going to the secondhand stores or would you rather look for something new?"

Bridget snapped out of her marriage musings. "I'd like to check out the secondhand designs. Maybe I'll find something that's actually from the Old Hollywood era."

Candy added carrots and cucumbers to a bowl of

leafy greens. "That's what I was thinking, too. Some of the stores categorize the clothes by whatever decade they're from to make it easier to shop. My friend's dress was from the seventies."

"Was it a traditional wedding dress from that era?" Bridget asked, curious about the bride.

"No. It was just something she wanted to get married in. She's really into vintage style. Her name is Dana, and she used to be my tenant."

"Your tenant?"

"In the guesthouse where you're staying. In fact, that was where she was living when she first dated Eric, the man who became her husband. He's also the one who reintroduced me to Tanner. He and Tanner are old friends."

"Eric and Dana must be really nice people."

"They are. I hosted their wedding, here, in my garden. But that was before Eric reintroduced me to Tanner. He and Tanner had lost touch over the years, then ran into each other about the time I was selling this house."

"That was good timing." Something that was clearly meant to be. "Or fate or whatever causes the stars to align like that."

"Yes, it was." Candy continued her tale. "Guess what else happened here? Dana and Eric's son. He was conceived in the guesthouse on their very first date. Dana always tells people that story. She's very free about what she says."

"My grandmother is like that, too. She never holds back." Bridget glanced out the glass door that led to the yard. "A lot of romantic things have occurred on this property."

"That's for sure. I never would have predicted it, though. Before I lived here, I went through a terrible divorce. I was even pregnant and had a miscarriage."

"Oh, my goodness, I'm so sorry." Bridget hadn't considered that the other woman's past might've been sad or tragic. She'd just assumed that someone with her glamorous background had lived a charmed life. "I had no idea. You just seem so—"

"Lucky? I am now, but I wasn't always. I had a difficult youth, with my mom pushing me to be so perfect. Tanner was my salvation when we were teenagers, and after he broke up with me, I rebounded with a man who controlled everything I did, just like my mother used to do."

"That sounds awful."

"Losing the baby was devastating, the worst thing I've ever endured. But now I have Tanner and Ivy and my whole future ahead of me. I made peace with my mother, as well. You should see the way she spoils Ivy."

"My family spoils Cody, too. They adored him from the moment he was born."

Candy leaned against the counter, her gaze locking onto Bridget's. "How do they feel about Kade?"

She responded honestly. "My grandma appreciates him, but my mom doesn't. Kade reminds her of my father. He roamed from place to place, too, until he just stopped coming around. I don't know if my mother will ever trust Kade. I'm just starting to trust him myself."

"Things can get complicated, especially when you have a preconceived notion about someone. Or a painful history that keeps rearing its head. There are a lot of factors that come into play. But it's obvious how attracted you and Kade are to each other."

Denying the truth wasn't an option. "We're sort of to-gether again. That's why he wants to take me on a date."

"I figured as much. I think you're going to have a wonderful time."

"Thank you. I think so, too." In spite of the wedding foolishness that had invaded her mind, Bridget wanted to get dressed up and dance and be dreamy. She was eager for the ball to arrive.

Dressed in a classic black tuxedo, Kade sat in Tan-ner's living room, waiting for Bridget. She was down the hall, getting ready for their date. Candy had offered to help do her hair and makeup, and the process seemed as if it was taking forever.

Tanner and Cody came into the room and plopped down in front of the TV. They had plans of their own, with movies they were going to stream and popcorn they intended to eat. Cody would be staying there to-night, of course, instead of coming back to the guest-house, and he was excited about his sleepover. Kade knew the feeling.

Cody glanced over at him. "You look nice, Dad."

"Thanks." He was doing his best not to tug at his tie or seem anxious about waiting.

"Yeah, he looks nice." Tanner smirked. "All buttoned up in a monkey suit."

Kade rolled his eyes. Trust his brother to poke fun at him. "What do you know about it?"

"I know a six-foot-four gorilla when I see one."

"Ha-ha. Funny guy. But you need to get your pri-mates straight. Gorillas aren't monkeys."

"I know, but you're too big to be a monkey. And if the costume fits…" He gestured to Kade's attire.

Cody listened to their banter, watching them like a tennis match. Then he asked, "Why are you calling it a monkey suit?"

Tanner replied, "Because that's slang for tuxedos."

"Yes, but why?"

"Hmm." Tanner furrowed his brow. "I never really thought about the origin." He shifted to Kade. "Have you?"

"Not especially, no. But let's find out." To uncover the answer, he got online with his phone, reading the information that popped up. "Some sites say it's because men's formal wear used to resemble the suits worn by monkeys that performed with organ grinders. Other sites make reference to *monkey jackets*, which is a term for waist-length jackets that were typically worn by sailors. There are other theories, too, but those are the most common."

Tanner grinned. "I like the organ grinder one the best."

"Me, too," Cody said, with the same goofy grin as his uncle. "It's funny to think of Dad dressed like that."

Kade was tempted to scratch his armpit and mimic the animal in question, but he didn't want Bridget coming into the room and catching him doing something so stupid.

Good thing, too. She appeared a few minutes later, with Candy by her side. And damn if Bridget wasn't a stunning sight to behold. Kade stood and stared at her.

She wore a sleek satin gown that hugged every luscious curve and exposed a ladylike hint of cleavage. She carried a shimmery gold evening bag. Her high-heeled shoes were gold, too. Over her shoulders was a short, intricately laced, delicately beaded wrap the same ivory color as the dress.

Her long, loose hair looked even shinier than usual, spilling around her face in thick waves. Her eyes were softly lined, and her ruby-red lips were as bold and brazen as sin.

"You look incredible," he said.

"Thank you," she told him. "So do you."

Bewitched by her transformation, he took an eager step toward her. "You're like a pinup come to life."

She touched a hand to her hair. Even her nails were painted red. "Candy used a picture of Veronica Lake to model my appearance after because I told her that you said I resembled her."

"It's an amazing likeness." Bridget was as sultry as any movie siren who'd ever graced the big screen.

Cody asked, "Is that really you, Mom?"

She smiled at their son. "Yes, it's me. Candy is a miracle worker."

Tanner's fiancée rebutted the claim. "That isn't true. Your mom is a natural beauty, Cody. I just helped her enhance what was already there."

Kade couldn't quit staring at her. Bridget had been his physical ideal from the day he'd first met her, and now she was his Old Hollywood fantasy, too.

"My dress is from the thirties," she said. "I tried to find something from the forties since that was Veronica Lake's heyday, but there weren't as many gowns available from that era because it was the height of the war years." She traced the laced edge of her wrap. "This capelet is from the twenties and was made in France. There's a row of beads missing, but that doesn't matter to me."

It didn't matter to him, either. As far as he was concerned, every detail was perfection. "You chose just the right outfit." He couldn't wait to be alone with her, to touch and kiss and dance. "Even your hair seems so much brighter, as if it's been streaked by the sun."

She ran her hands through the blond strands, letting them fall where they may. "Candy used a natural rinse on it made from flowers and herbs to create that effect."

Kade wanted to luxuriate in her hair, too, as he'd done on the night they'd made fast-paced love. Only this time, he wouldn't be so harsh as to tangle it. "You're going to be the most gorgeous woman at the ball."

"I don't know about that." A pair of dangling rhinestones glittered at her ears. "But this is certainly the prettiest I've ever felt."

"I have a corsage for you in the fridge." He glanced back at the kitchen. "It's a red carnation. I asked Candy ahead of time if red works with what you were going to wear, and she said it would." And now he knew why, considering Bridget's lips and nails.

"I'll go get it," Tanner said, when Kade couldn't seem to walk away from his date.

His brother left the room, and then returned with a clear plastic box. Kade removed the ribbon-wrapped corsage and attached it to Bridget's wrist.

"It means *fascination*," he told her. He knew because he'd looked it up.

"Is that why you chose this type of flower?" she asked.

He nodded. He wanted something that would symbolize his feelings for her. "Yes, that's exactly why."

"It's beautiful," she replied, sounding as fascinated by him as he was by her. "Thank you."

"You're welcome." He'd made sure that the carnation was a light shade of red because the depth of the color mattered. The language of flowers, he'd discovered, was far more complex than it seemed. Much like the woman he was taking to the ball.

The big, opulent hotel was located in the heart of Beverly Hills and surrounded by palm trees and tropical foliage, with a posh history connected to Old Hollywood.

Bridget could almost see them, these famous ghosts from the past—men with flirtatious voices and pencil-thin moustaches, women wrapped in furs and dripping in diamonds, posing with long, slim cigarette holders. In her mind's eye, they breezed through the party, swishing the air.

Not that there weren't plenty of flesh-and-blood people in attendance, draped in glamorous gowns and glitzy jewels. Bridget should have been out of her element. Yet here she was, walking around in vintage clothes with a sinfully hot man on her arm, as if she was a natural part of the setting, where tea-light candles floated in the pool and stars twinkled in the sky.

"Do you want a glass of champagne?" Kade asked. "Or would you rather try something you've never had before?"

"I like the idea of something new." Especially on a night like this. "Do you have any suggestions for a sexy cocktail?"

He leaned closer. "Sexy?"

She breathed in his cologne, letting his warm, woodsy scent engulf her. "Or fancy or whatever."

"Too late to backpedal. You already said sexy."

"Then, help me choose one." She fluttered her lashes, teasing him with a coy look. "Something decadent."

He smiled. "Are you sure you want me to do that? I'm not an authority on this subject. We could just ask the bartender."

"I'd rather have it come from you."

"I can't guarantee that you'll like the taste or even what the ingredients are. All I know are the sexy names I've heard bandied about."

"That will work." She just wanted to have some fun.

"How about Sex on the Beach?"

She scrunched up her nose. "That's too common. Everybody always talks about that one."

"Okay, then maybe you can have an Orgasm? Or a Screaming Orgasm."

She laughed and smacked his shoulder. The big gorgeous brute. "I'm not drinking either of those."

He laughed, too, his voice deliciously gruff. "Sorry. But I warned you I wasn't an authority."

She prompted him to keep going. She wasn't going to let it end that easily. "Come on, try again, but with something that leaves a bit more to the imagination."

"Can I do an internet search?"

She shook her head. "That would be cheating. You have to do this on your own."

"Then, give me a minute." He slid his gaze up and down her dress. Lavishly. Meticulously.

Was he using her body for inspiration? Bridget refused to get shy. This was her game, after all, and she liked that he was infatuated with her. She hadn't told him that she was wearing silk stockings and a garter belt. Part of the thrill was letting him find out on his own.

"I've got it," he said.

She sucked in her breath. "You do?"

"Yes. You can have a Between the Sheets, and I'll have a Seduction on the Rocks."

"You're having a sexy drink, too?"

"Sure, why not? I'm up for trying something different. And it'll be interesting to see if I made the right choices."

She readily agreed. "Then, let's go for it."

Bridget waited while he worked his way through the crowd and approached the nearest bar. As she watched him, she marveled at his power and masculine grace. She noticed that he was turning other women's heads, too. But he always did, no matter what environment he was in.

He came back with the drinks and handed her a cocktail garnished with a twist of lemon.

"Here you go," he said. "Between the Sheets."

"Thank you. It looks lovely." She took a sip, and her taste buds exploded with a wonderful burst of citrus. "It's good. I like it, but other than lemon juice, I can't tell what's in it."

"I asked the bartender, and according to him it's a combination of brandy and rum. He also said that it's been around since the Prohibition era. Oh, and that there's another drink similar to it called Maiden's Prayer, except with gin as the base. It's a Prohibition drink, too."

"Ooh. Can I have one of those next?"

"Why? So you can become a maiden between the sheets?"

"Touché." She smiled, feeling smart and sassy. "That's what I was when I first met you."

He teased her. "Until I stole your virtue?"

"You didn't steal it. I gave it to you." She gestured to his Seduction on the Rocks. "What's in yours?"

"Orange juice, butterscotch liqueur and lemon-lime soda."

"That sounds good, too."

He clanked her glass. "To sexy drinks and sexy women."

She studied him, taking in his broad shoulders and debonair suit. "You forgot sexy men."

He accepted her toast and swigged his cocktail. Then he set his glass on the ledge of a brick planter next to where they stood. He removed Bridget's drink from her hand and placed it beside his.

"I'm not finished yet," she said.

"I'm not done with mine, either."

"Then, why did you put them there?"

"So they won't get in the way when I kiss you."

She caught her breath. "In front of all these people?"

"No one is paying attention."

"They will be if we start kissing." Indulging in naughtily named drinks was one thing, but locking lips in a crowd was quite another. She glanced over her shoulder, toward a shroud of trees. "We should go over there."

"I don't want to slip off to a darkened corner. I want to stay here, with the moon reflecting off the pool. What's the point of being in such a pretty place if we don't take advantage of it?"

She fussed with her wrap, covering the tops of her breasts. Now she wished that she'd worn a high-neck dress. She wondered if she'd made a mistake with the color, too. If ivory was too bridal. "As long as you don't overdo it."

"I won't."

"Are you sure?"

"Yes, I'm sure. I won't disrespect you in public."

She wet her lips. "Maybe we should have ordered drinks that had kisses in the names."

"That wouldn't have worked, not as a substitute. Nothing is going to work, except doing it for real."

She moved toward him, struggling to stay steady on her feet. Suddenly her shoes felt too high, the heels too spiky.

He leaned into her, his lips lightly touching hers.

Immersed in the sensation, she sighed in sweet bliss. Now that his mouth was gently fused to hers, she teetered on the feeling. He tasted as daring as the cocktails they'd sipped.

She moaned and pressed closer, trying desperately not to think of him as her groom. This was just one night. One romantic date. Not a lifetime of togetherness.

But that didn't stop her from wanting more…

She could tell that he wanted more, too. He held her tightly against his body, sliding his fingers along the zipper on her dress. But all too soon, he kept his word, backing away before he went too far.

She blinked at him, every cell in her body on alert. "It's over already?" They'd barely used their tongues.

"Yes, and I don't think anyone even saw us."

Or if they did, they didn't care. She dropped her gaze to his mouth. "You got some of my lipstick on you."

"I did?" He wiped the back of his hand across his mouth and came away with a mark that looked like blood.

"I should have blotted a little better."

"Is that what women do when they wear dark lip-stick?"

"It's what Candy told me to do. I've never worn any-thing this dark before. I brought the tube with me in case I needed to reapply it after dinner." She was still stumbling from the kiss. "Do I need to fix it now?"

"No. It didn't get messed up."

"It's not smeared? Not even a little?"

He shook his head. "It's perfect, Bridget."

"I guess I used you as my blotter, then."

He smiled. "Feel free anytime." He removed their cocktails from the ledge and handed hers back. "What's it called?"

"What's what called?"

"Your lipstick."

"I can't remember." Her brain wasn't working right. "Do you want me to check?"

"No, that's okay. You can check later, when you need to reapply it. Until then, I'll just enjoy the way it looks on you."

"Can I ask you something, Kade?"

"Of course. You can ask me anything."

"Have you ever done this before?"

He polished off his drink, leaving the ice spinning in his glass. "Done what?"

"Been on this kind of date, where it's so elegant and whatnot."

"I've been to black-tie events before. Some of my clients have high-end parties, but I've never brought a date. Normally I prefer to go stag."

She liked knowing that no one had come before her,

at least not at a gala like this. It was already turning out to be the most enchanted evening she'd ever had.

And it had only just begun.

Chapter Twelve

Kade and Bridget wandered around the portion of the ballroom where the silent auction was being held. Costumes that had been worn by famous stars were up for bid and so were movie props used in some of the classic old B films. Less expensive things, including framed posters and signed pictures, could be had, as well.

Kade searched for an autographed photo of Veronica Lake, but he couldn't find one. He discovered a signed eight-by-ten glossy of Roy Rogers and Dale Evans, though.

"Maybe Dale really is my kindred spirit," Bridget said.

Kade studied the image of Roy in his decorative Western garb. "Maybe he's mine, too. But without the silver spurs and foot-long fringe." Kade wouldn't be caught dead in a singing-cowboy outfit.

"They looked like a happy couple." Bridget read the biography that accompanied their picture. "It says that they were married for fifty-one years." She kept reading. "Oh, this is sad. They had a daughter with Down syndrome who died when she was a toddler. She was their only biological child together. The rest were adopted or were from previous marriages."

"Does it say what their daughter's name was?"

"No. But Dale wrote a book about it during a time when it was taboo to discuss special-needs children." Bridget glanced up from the biography. "He was more than just the king of cowboys, and she was more than just the queen of the West. They were real people with real lives who tried to make a difference in the world."

Touched by Bridget's assessment of the couple, Kade said, "I'm going to bid on their picture."

"You are?"

He nodded and wrote his bid on the sheet that had been provided. "I'll come back and check on it before it closes." And raise the amount, if necessary. "But if I win the bid, you have to promise to put the picture in your house. Or in your barn, if you prefer. Just pick a place where it seems to fit."

"Oh, my. You're getting it for me?"

"You want it, don't you?"

"Yes. Absolutely. It's interesting, too, that they died within just a few years of each other." She referred to the biography again. "He passed away in 1998, and she followed in 2001."

"I wasn't aware of who went first." Kade knew quite a bit about Roy's beloved palomino, though. "Did you know that after Trigger died, Roy had his hide stretched and mounted over a likeness of the horse rearing on its hind legs? He was kept on display in Roy and Dale's museum until it closed. Trigger was the main attraction. People loved going there to see him."

"I hate to say this, but I can't imagine stuffing one of my horses."

"I know, it does seem a little weird, but taxidermy was more common back then, and it was probably just Roy's way of honoring him. That horse was brilliant. He could react to hundreds of cues and could walk up to fifty feet on his hind legs. He had a kind and gentle nature, too. He and Roy would visit sick children in hospitals, with Roy on his back, the two of them bounding up flights of stairs to get to the kids."

She touched her hand against her heart. "Oh, that's sweet."

"Trigger had his own fan club. He also had his own comic book and lunch pail. That's some memorabilia I wouldn't mind getting hold of."

She smiled. "Yes, I can see how much you admire him."

"What can I say? He was a damned fine horse."

"Why didn't Trigger ever get his own star?"

"I don't know, but his hoofprints are on the same square as Roy's handprints and footprints in front of the Chinese Theatre, so he's still a big part of the Walk of Fame." Which still remained on their vacation itinerary. "I was thinking we could go there tomorrow."

"That sounds great. I'm sure Cody will be up for it."

"Yeah. Our kid loves the Hollywood thing."

"I do, too, apparently." She gestured to her glamorous attire. "Who knew I would ever get fixed up like this?"

"You really are the most gorgeous woman here." He

offered her his arm and escorted her to the dining room, where dinner was about to be served.

Bridget gazed at the dessert bar. She couldn't get over how many flaky, creamy, frothy, spongy treats were available.

They'd already had a prime-rib meal with all the trimmings, and now they were being offered a stunning assortment of sweets.

"This is heavenly," she said. "But I don't know what to get."

Kade stood beside her, waiting for her to decide. "You can sample as many as you want."

"That would be greedy." She narrowed it down. "Maybe I'll just take two." She reached for a glass goblet of chocolate mousse. For her next selection, she chose a cream puff covered with powdered sugar.

Kade went for two, as well. He took a piece of red velvet cake and a slice of lemon chiffon pie.

Bridget eyed his choices. "Those look good."

He leaned in close and whispered, "Don't worry. We can share."

They returned to their table, which was positioned near a window with a view of the pool. Bridget tasted her mousse and moaned.

Kade raised his eyebrows and said, "Maybe you should have had one of the Orgasm drinks."

She shot him a cheeky smile. "I don't need one, not with all of this chocolate."

"That does look like an aphrodisiac." He ate a forkful of his pie. "But this is, too."

She didn't doubt it. Kade offered her a taste of the lemon chiffon and she accepted it willingly. She, in turn, cut into her cream puff and let him try it. They went back and forth, enjoying the shared experience.

After nearly every bite was gone, they sat quietly, sipping cups of mint-flavored tea.

Then Kade said, "I'm going to the auction area to check on my bid."

"That's fine. I'll go fix my lipstick." By now, she'd probably wiped most of it off on her napkin.

They headed in different directions, and she glanced back to see him disappear into the crowd.

Once she reached her destination, she entered the lavishly decorated parlor of the ladies' room and approached a gilded mirror.

Surrounded by other elegantly dressed women, she applied the color, then blotted carefully, so that the next time she and Kade kissed, she wouldn't get it on him. She also glanced at the tube to see the name so she could tell him what it was.

After she dropped the lipstick back into her chic little 1920s bag, she stayed in front of the mirror, barely recognizing her own reflection. Who was she, this glamorous blonde looking back at her? When the answer came to her, she smiled.

A Montana Cinderella at a Beverly Hills ball.

Thankfully, though, she wasn't going to dash off at midnight and lose one of her glittery gold shoes. This ball would end with Cinderella sleeping in the cowboy prince's bed.

She returned to the table and saw that Kade had returned, as well.

"I won this bid," he said happily. "They're going to send the picture to you. I gave them your home address. It comes with a certificate of authenticity."

"Thank you. That's wonderful. I can't wait to display it." To keep it as a memento of this magical date. She waited a beat before she said, "By the way, my lipstick is called Splash of Red."

"Oh, I like that." He glanced at her mouth, and then looked into her eyes. "Dance with me, Bridget. Dance with me so I can kiss you again."

She wanted to kiss him, too, and she didn't care who saw them. He escorted her onto the dance floor, where other couples had already begun to sway to an old-time tune being sung by a male vocalist with a bluesy voice.

"What's this song called?" she asked.

"'As Time Goes By.'" He took her in his arms. "It's from the movie *Casablanca*."

"Is that one with Humphrey Bogart and—" She couldn't think of the woman's name.

"Ingrid Bergman. It's where the 'Play it again, Sam' line came from. Only he never actually said it that way. He just says, 'Play it, Sam.'"

"And he's referring to this song?"

"Yes. Haven't you ever seen *Casablanca*?"

"No." As they glided to the music, she asked, "Is it the same movie where he says, 'Here's looking at you, kid'?"

Kade nodded. "But supposedly that line wasn't in the original screenplay. It's something Bogart said to Bergman in between takes while he was teaching her to play poker. So they wrote it into the movie."

"That's a nice story."

"It's a powerful movie. We should watch it together sometime."

"I'd like that." She really liked the song, too, as tragic as it seemed. The lyrics were romantic, but somehow painful. "Were Bogart and Bergman a couple in real life?"

"No. He was married to Lauren Bacall. She was the love of his life."

"Oh, that's right. I got them mixed up." Bridget wasn't an Old Hollywood aficionado the way Kade was. But she was getting there, learning as she went. "Do the characters in *Casablanca* end up together?"

"You don't want me to give away the plot, do you?"

"No, I suppose not." But she suspected that it wasn't a happily-ever-after story, not if the lyrics to the theme song were an indication of how the film played out.

Kade lowered his mouth to hers and kissed her softly. She moved closer to him, wanting to feel his heartbeat.

After the song ended, Bridget put her hand against her lover's cheek, wishing he would kiss her again.

A female vocalist took the microphone, and the band started playing "Over the Rainbow."

Kade smiled and said, "Now, don't you dare tell me that you haven't seen the movie this is from."

She laughed, a little dreamily, thinking about Dorothy and her crew. When Bridget was little, she used to imagine being swept into a make-believe tornado. "Yes, I've seen *The Wizard of Oz*. I don't know if Cody has, though."

"Really? Now, that's just crazy. Every kid should see it, especially ours."

"I'll make sure that he sees it in the future."

"I'm glad that you're his mother."

"And I'm glad that you're his dad." Eager for the warmth of Kade's mouth, she initiated the next kiss. But neither of them made it too deep or too sexy. They would save that for later when they were alone.

* * *

They stayed until the ball ended, and in the wee hours of the morning, they returned to the guesthouse, with Bridget still feeling the effects of having danced half the night away in Kade's arms.

He led her to his room and turned down the lights. While she placed her wrap on a chair, he removed his jacket and tie. Both of them took off their shoes and tucked them out of the way.

With his gaze fixed on hers, he sat on the edge of the bed and said, "I want to watch you undress all the way."

Bridget's heart skipped a sensual beat. "You have to help me unzip my gown." She couldn't do it on her own.

"Then, come closer."

She moved over to where he was, then stood with her back to him. "There's a little eyehook at the very top." She lifted her hair off her neck.

"I see it." He unlatched the hook and slid the zipper halfway down. "Can you get it from here?"

"Yes." She reached around to undo the remaining portion, letting him watch. As soon as it was open, she turned to face him.

Since the front of her dress was loose, she lowered the fabric and let it pool on the floor, showcasing her carefully chosen underwear.

"Damn," he said. "I didn't know... I hadn't expected... I mean, really, damn. How beautiful are you?"

"I was hoping you'd like it." She wore a modern bra and itty-bitty panties with an old-fashioned garter belt and silk stockings. She made a full circle, turning like a ballerina on top of a jewelry box, letting him see every angle. Now wasn't the time to be shy.

"I wonder what flowers I would have to give you to say how impressed I am."

"I don't know." She glanced at the corsage on her wrist. "But I like the one I have." It represented the fascination that rippled between them. "Should I keep going?"

"Yes, please. Take everything off."

She started with her bra, exposing her breasts. Her nipples were already pearling into pink nubs, sensitive to the lust in the air. He didn't reach out to touch, even if it was obvious that he wanted to, even as he kept flexing his fingers.

In order to remove her stockings, she sat next to Kade and undid the clasps, rolling the hosiery down each leg.

"You do that well." He kept watching, keeping a close eye on her. "Like the ladies back in the day."

"I feel like one of them." She peeled off her panties. Tonight she was a pinup girl, or as close to one as she knew how to be. Naked, she reclined on the bed, keeping her legs in a modest pose. Curious about the actress who inspired her appearance, she asked, "Who was Veronica Lake linked with? Who was the man in her life?"

Still dressed in his shirt and pants, Kade leaned over and aligned his body with hers. "As far as I know, she wasn't linked with anyone specific. I think she was married and divorced a number of times."

"Did she have a leading man in the movies?"

"She made films with Alan Ladd. She was known for being a femme fatale in those." He lowered his head, stealing a hot, sweet kiss.

Steeped in the gentleness of his touch, she moaned against his lips. He'd insisted that he was going to go slow tonight, to be romantic, and he was doing just that. Bridget's eyelids fluttered, and her pulse danced like stones skimming along a stream.

He kissed his way down her body, moving at a silky pace.

"What are you doing to me?" she asked, even though she knew. His mouth was between her legs now.

She glided her hands through his hair and let him have his luscious way with her. Heat swirled through her body, drawing her into his spell, taking her to the edge of his world.

She could have said his name a thousand times. This whirlwind of a man. This tuxedoed cowboy. This magic drifter.

Kade... Kade... Kade...

While he worked his bewitchment, desire seeped through her pores, twining into colors that misted before her eyes. Lost in the feeling, she arched like Cupid's bow and convulsed into a prism of passion.

He gave her a moment to clear her vision, to catch what was left of her runaway breath, before he discarded the remainder of his clothes and pressed his nakedness against hers.

Kade looked at Bridget, making sure she was looking at him, too. After everything they'd done tonight— the drinking, the kissing, the flirting, the dancing—he wanted her to hold his gaze while he pushed deep inside.

"The maiden between the sheets," he said.

Reacting to his words, she dragged him down for a kiss. As their mouths came together, he rolled over so that she was on top.

With her straddling him good and tight, they continued the kiss. The fire. The excitement.

Once they came up for air, she rode him, with her hair falling forward and blanketing the sides of her face.

He grasped a handful of the billowing blondness and noticed that she still wore her earrings, the rhinestones shimmering like diamonds.

She moved up and down, soft and sleek and womanly. But there was friction, too, the kind that came with the joining of aroused flesh.

Kade couldn't imagine not ever being with her again. Yet there were no promises between them, at least not in a way that allowed him to claim her.

Was that what he wanted? To keep her as his own?

To stop himself from analyzing his thoughts, he focused on the sex. That was all that mattered for now. Her smooth skin and rounded curves. The scent of her. The feel of her. The pleasures she provided.

"You should let me decorate your body," he said, circling her waist. "I could draw pretty pictures on you."

"Maybe I could just use temporary tattoos instead."

"What would you use? What designs?"

"Maybe I'd get a flower." She kept moving, impaling herself on him, over and over. "Or maybe I'd get your name."

His name? That sounded crazy and sexy and dangerously impulsive. "You'd brand yourself like that?"

"Temporary tattoos come off."

Yes, of course. They weren't talking about the genuine thing. "Then, I'd get one with your name, too." Just to help satisfy the craving. "Bridget." He envisioned the letters on his skin. "Right here." He showed her the spot where he would put it, against the muscle on his biceps.

"I'd put mine here." She pressed a finger to her inner thigh, delicately close to her nether region.

Kade's heart punched the hell out of his chest. "I think you really are turning into a femme fatale."

She bit down on her Splash of Red lips. "For now I am."

Taking control once again, he switched positions, so that he was back on top.

"Why did you do that?" she asked as she sank her head onto a pillow, her hair spilling over the crisp cotton pillowcase. "Don't you like me being on top?"

He cuffed her wrists with his hands, nearly knocking the corsage loose as he pinned her to the bed. "Maybe I'm just taking what's mine. For tonight," he added, reminding himself that claiming possession of her was temporary, like the fake tattoos that could be washed away.

Releasing her from his bonds, he set an erotic rhythm, giving her the freedom to move with him. They absorbed each other, taking, giving, savoring the feeling of being together.

The gasps. The moans. The hot, slick penetration. Everything was melding and becoming one.

Kade thrust into her one last time, ready and willing to let himself fall, just as he saw it happening to her, too.

She wrapped her legs around him, holding tight, riding out the sweet storm that rained over them.

In the next pulse-pounding minute, he withdrew, and they lay side by side, their fingertips touching.

As natural as could be, she rolled over and into his arms. He kissed the top of her head. "Are you going to sleep in your makeup?"

She nibbled at his shoulder. "I might."

But before the night was through, they both got up to get ready for bed. They went into the bathroom and took turns brushing their teeth. He stood back from the sink while she scrubbed her face.

"Now I'm back to being me," she said, leaving her earrings on the counter. "No more femme fatale." She put the corsage there, too, treating it carefully.

He eyed the flower. "After all of the abuse that took, you're worried about it now?"

"It still has its petals." She smoothed the ribbon. "Besides, I'm going to keep it."

And preserve it as a memory? Oddly enough, he liked the idea, overly girlish as it was. But she'd warned him that the femme fatale was gone.

They returned to his room and got under the covers. She curled up, cozy as you please, and purred like a contented cat. Kade turned out the light and drew her closer to him, allowing her to drift into a protected slumber, while he stayed awake and listened to her breathe.

Chapter Thirteen

The forecourt of the Chinese Theatre had nearly two hundred celebrity footprints, handprints and autographs in the cement, and Kade was happy to show them to Bridget and his son, to be their tour guide.

While Cody ran around, putting his hands and feet in the impressions and pretending that he was a star, Kade and Bridget approached Roy and Trigger's square of sidewalk. He'd seen it on other occasions, but this time he noticed something that hadn't mattered before: the April 21, 1949, date that had been written in the cement.

"That's Cody's birthday," he said, pointing out the obvious. "Not the year, of course, but the month and day."

She quickly replied, "Yes, it most certainly is. How strange is that?"

He knelt and glided his hand across the date. Bridget

had put a copy of Cody's birth certificate in the time capsule, but Kade had never expected it to be the same day, many years before, that Roy and Trigger had made their impressions. "This makes it even more special that you and Cody took this trip with me."

She knelt beside him. "I think so, too."

He glanced in their son's direction. Cody looked like the ultimate California tourist in his Legoland cap and Mickey Mouse T-shirt.

Bridget traced Trigger's horseshoed hoofprints. "It's almost over, though. Just a few more days."

Kade nodded. Their vacation was nearly done. In fact, it would be ending with a visit to the prison to see his sister, something he'd been uncomfortable about since the start.

Trying to stay focused on the here and now, he returned his attention to the square. Along with handprints and footprints, Roy had also made an impression of his revolver in the cement.

"This is a nice piece of history," she said, "especially with the connection to Cody's birthday. But I don't think I would have felt as attached to it if we hadn't attended the ball or if you hadn't bought me the autographed picture."

Sharing all of that with her had made a difference for Kade, too. "And look whose prints are right above these. Humphrey Bogart."

"You're right." She reached forward to touch the shape of Bogie's hand. "Another reminder of the ball. And the movie we're supposed to watch." She leaned back. "What's really going to happen when we return to our regular lives?"

He gave her a puzzled look. "What do you mean?"

"Are we going to keep seeing each other the way we are now? Going on dates and sleeping together?"

He thought about how she'd affected him last night when they were in bed, the mixed-up feeling of wanting to keep her. "Is that what you want to do?"

She nodded, albeit shakily. "I'd hate for this to be just some sort of vacation fling. But I don't want to repeat my mother's mistakes, to sit around with bated breath, waiting for my lover to come to town."

"I wouldn't want you to do that, either. If we keep this going, it doesn't have to be like your parents. I wouldn't drift in and out of your life or leave you on a string. I'd stay in proper touch with you."

"But you wouldn't settle down or stop traveling?"

"That's not who I am, Bridget."

Silent, she remained on her knees. He stayed where he was, too.

Finally she said, "It scares me."

"I know. It scares me, too." The emotional impact, the pressure, the differences in their lifestyles. "We shouldn't even be talking about this. I think we should just forget it."

"Forget it?" Her voice vibrated. "And do what? See other people?"

Kade frowned, the notion of her being with another guy causing him to clench his gut. "I meant let the conversation go." He scanned her expression. "Why? Do you want to be free to date other men?"

She stared at him, her frown seeming as deep and troubled as his. "Why? Are you interested in other women?"

"Not in the least." Why in the hell would he want

someone else when he could have her? "You're the one who brought it up. Why did you even say it?"

"Because I was confused about what you wanted."

Cripes, he thought. He didn't know what he wanted, other than keeping her to himself and away from other men. "Maybe we should just agree to be together."

"Even if it scares us?"

"It's better than analyzing it to death."

"What if we can't handle it?"

"Then, we can end it. I'm not saying that either of us will be able to do it forever. But what harm is there in trying and seeing how long it lasts?"

"Okay," she said, her chest rising and falling in an audible breath. "We can try it."

Relief shot through his blood, along with a hefty dose of fear. In that sense, he was as mixed up as ever.

Nonetheless, he reached out to caress her cheek, and she leaned into his hand, the affection creating a warm and caring feeling. If they'd been alone, he would've kissed her. But they had a child to consider.

"Should we tell Cody that we're going to keep dating?" Kade asked, letting his fingers drift from her cheek. "Seems to me he should be made aware of it."

She nodded. "I think so, too."

"Then, let's tell him now."

They both got up and headed over to their son.

"Hey, you guys," Cody said. "Did you see that one over there, with the Harry Potter kids? It's my favorite. They even put impressions of their wands in it."

"That's great, honey," Bridget replied, before she glanced at Kade. "But your father has something he wants to say." Clearly, she was going to let him put it in his own words.

"What's up?" Cody asked, turning to look at him.

Kade got right to the point, even if his pulse had decided to kick its way to his throat. "You know how your mom and I went out last night? Well, we agreed that we're going to keep dating and try to be a couple. It'll be a long-distance relationship, with us seeing each other when I come to visit."

Cody's eyes went big and wide. "You're Mom's boyfriend now?"

Kade wouldn't have thought to define it that way. But it sounded simple enough, coming from a ten-year-old. "Sure, I suppose you could say that."

"Oh, man." The boy made a happy little bunny hop. "You can go on as many dates as you want. I swear, I won't get in your way."

Kade put his hand on his son's shoulder. "Are you kidding? You'd never be in the way. Without you, there would be no us."

"I'm so excited." Cody jumped around again. "You and Mom are going to be together, almost like other parents."

Yes, almost, Kade thought. Most other parents would be married and living under the same roof. But he wasn't going to dwell on that. He had enough to cope with already.

Bridget agreed to let Kade stay in her room. With Cody knowing the truth, there didn't seem to be any reason to sleep separately. Still, she fidgeted with the edge of the sheet, tugging it up and down while she and Kade lay side by side, staring at the ceiling.

"Stop being so anxious," he said. "You're making me nervous, too."

She couldn't stop thinking about the arrangement they'd made, the hasty decision to remain together, to make it official. "It just seems like such a risky step we're taking."

He rolled over to face her. "Why? Because you don't think we're cut out to be boyfriend and girlfriend?"

She couldn't help but laugh, hearing Kade use Cody's term. "That makes us sound like teenagers."

"I know." Kade laughed a bit, too. "But the truth is, I've never been anyone's boyfriend until now."

She suspected as much, given his nature. But she questioned him anyway. "What about in high school?"

"Nope, not even then. I dated a few girls, but it never amounted to anything. I did get laid for the first time during that era. I didn't go to school with her, though. She was a little older than I was. But I'd prefer not to share the details."

"That's fine." She accepted his right to remain silent. "Gentlemen aren't supposed to kiss and tell." And she didn't want to think about him with someone else anyway.

He shifted onto his elbow. "I don't see where high school counts all that much. Some kids become long-lasting sweethearts, but most teenage relationships don't even get past the first few weeks."

"My longest was two months, and that was a big ordeal for me. *Zack Parker.*" She recited his name in a silly, girlie voice. "I cried like a baby when he broke up with me, and I didn't even have very strong feelings for him."

"So it was the rejection you were crying over?"

"It hurt to be dumped." Plus she'd associated it with

her dad leaving. Everything for her always came back to that.

"Where's Zack now?"

"I have no idea. He left town a long time ago."

Kade touched a strand of her hair. "You seem to get tangled up with men who don't want to sit still."

"Zack was a boy when I knew him, not a man. And he never mattered." Not like Kade. Still, she couldn't let him become her entire world, or let herself start living and breathing for every moment that he came to town. Bridget couldn't behave like her mother or let Kade behave like her father. There were already too many similarities. The prospect of a long-distance affair was hitting too close to home.

Before she let herself drown in fear, she asked, "What about when you were in college? How did you escape the girlfriend route then?"

"Truthfully? It was easier because there were a lot of women who just wanted to hook up or keep things casual. But I was still cautious about who my partners were. But you already know that I won't be with just anyone."

Bridget was that way, too, of course. She was able to control her urges, except with him, it seemed. "I'm glad you're going to be with just me now."

"Are you? For sure?"

"Yes." She moved into his arms, needing to be held, needing to convince herself everything would be all right.

He drew her closer. "I like that you belong to me. That I'm making you mine."

She inhaled the lingering scent of his cologne. "My new boyfriend."

"I'm going to be way better than Zack Parker." He glided a hand down her back. "And do you know how sexy this little getup of yours is?"

Bridget smiled. He was naked, but she was dressed in her pajama top and panties. "I have no idea what you're talking about. I'm a proper girl. Always was. Always will be."

"Oh, yeah?" He moved his other hand between their bodies. "Let's just see about that."

She gasped when he found his way into her panties, his fingers going deep. "I can't believe you just did that." She played along with his naughty game. "You're taking advantage of my innocence."

"Sorry, sweetheart, but that ship already sailed." He spoke softly, teasingly, his fingers working their magic. "And I was the captain."

"You still are." She closed her eyes and let him seduce her. He knew exactly what to do to make her melt.

"E-ono'aha."

She opened her eyes and looked at him, the unfamiliar word dancing in the air.

"It means, 'She is beautiful,'" he said.

"Am I?"

"Yes, very beautiful." He kissed her with hard-edged carnality.

She moaned, and it crackled from her throat, as rough as his kiss. He kept touching her, arousing her, toying with the spot that made her crazy. Pleasure zinged through her blood, through her half-clothed body.

She reacted, pressing her hips closer to his hand. Closer…closer…

His kiss turned gentle, then hard, then gentle again, making her thoughts spin. Her heart was spinning, too, all wrapped up with his, making her long for the kind of togetherness she could count on.

The kind that came with a ring and a vow?

Sakes alive! Warning herself not to think along those lines, Bridget did her damnedest to shut it out of her mind. Because her only obsession, the only thing she was going to focus on, was his touch. The way he was making her feel in the moment.

Kade walked beside his sister along the fenced perimeter of the prison patio. He tried to imagine that they were spending a lazy Sunday afternoon at the park, but everywhere he looked, there was a camera or a correctional officer or something to remind him that Meagan was a convict.

He'd never seen her in such drab clothes, but she couldn't help the uniform she was required to wear. He supposed she couldn't help looking so tired, either. He doubted that she'd been sleeping much. Nonetheless, he was struck by how much she resembled their mother, with her long, straight dark hair and liquid brown eyes.

He glanced toward the table where the rest of their family sat. Tanner and Candy were fussing over Ivy, and Bridget and Cody were playing a board game, with Cody munching on snacks that had come from a vending machine.

"I really like your son," Meagan said. "He's a super-great kid."

"Thank you. Your daughter is a sweetheart, too."

"Ivy is more than I could have hoped for." She tucked a loose strand of her ponytailed hair behind her ear. "Who would have ever guessed our lives would have turned out this way? With us having such wonderful children?"

He said what was on both of their minds. "Or having kids at all."

She stopped walking, turning to study him in the sunlight. "Mom used to worry about all of us—me being so flighty, Tanner with his playboy ways and you being so distant and alone. And now Tanner is engaged to Candy, and you've got a ten-year-old son and a—" She hesitated, waiting, it seemed, for him to fill in the blank.

"A girlfriend," he provided.

"Is that what Bridget is to you?"

"That's how Cody is defining it."

"She seems really genuine, as though she's a truly nice person. I'm glad you have someone, Kade, especially someone so good and kind." Meagan continued to study him. "Are you moving to Montana with her and Cody?"

He shook his head, a bit too quickly, too nervously. "It's not like that."

She frowned. "Then, how is it?"

"We're going for the long-distance approach, with me coming into town to see them when I can."

She tilted her head at a slight angle. "Really? That sounds kind of crappy to me. Not the way I would want it if I had a choice in the matter."

A blast of anger hit him. Guilt, too. Mounds of it. He knew it wasn't the way Bridget wanted it, either. "Don't judge me, Meagan."

"I'm just saying what I feel."

He defended himself. "What you feel isn't pertinent to my life."

She shrugged, sighed, blew out a breath. "It's just that after everything I've been through, I want things to be right for everyone else. And it's hard to imagine Bridget and Cody being happy seeing you on the fly."

"You don't know anything about it." Nor was he going to tell her. Because if she knew about the hell Bridget's dad had put her and her mom through, she would hold Kade even more responsible. "I love my son, and I—" his heart scrambled as he struggled to say how he felt about Bridget "—care about his mother, too."

"I'm sorry. You're right. I tried to push Tanner and Candy together before they were ready because I wanted them to adopt Ivy. Believe me, I'm the last person who should be doling out advice."

He took both of her hands in his, offering her his support. She was his kid sister, after all, the sweet little girl he'd barely known when she was growing up. "How do you feel about the adoption issue now?"

"Mostly I just worry that I could never be the kind of parent Ivy needs, that she would be better off with Tanner and Candy. But then when I think of giving her up, *really* giving her up, I can't bear the thought of losing her."

He squeezed her hands. "Just give yourself time to heal and work on getting rehabilitated. And for the record, you seem like a really good mom to me."

"I do?" Her gaze zeroed in on his.

"I saw the way you held your daughter, the way you made her smile and laugh. And the fact that you have her best interests at heart—whatever those turn out to be—says a lot about you as a parent."

"Thank you." She leaned in for a hug.

He wrapped his arms around her, and for one gentle instant, he forgot that they were standing in a prison yard.

They returned to the picnic table where the others were, and Meagan reached for Ivy and rocked her on her lap. Kade sat beside Bridget. Still playing the game with Cody, she glanced his way, sending him a soft smile.

Touched by how warm and uncharacteristically cozy she made him feel, he moved closer to her, hoping that their scattered relationship wasn't going to blow up in his face.

Chapter Fourteen

Both happy and sad to be back home in Montana, Bridget reclined on the living room sofa with her head in Kade's lap. They'd just finished lunch, and now they were listening to country music on the radio.

It should have been a nice, easy day. She should have been more relaxed than she was. Cody was at a friend's house, and she had Kade all to herself. But all she could think about was his upcoming jobs. He was leaving tomorrow to go to Wyoming so he could teach a weekend clinic. After that, he would return for a few weeks, and then head off to New Mexico to meet with a new client. From there, she had no idea when he would be back.

Bridget gazed at the fireplace mantel, where groupings of family photos were displayed. She'd put Roy and Dale's picture there, too, treating them like part of her clan.

"Their daughter's name was Robin," she said.

"What? Who?" he asked.

"The little girl Roy and Dale had who died."

"You read more about them?"

"Yes." She'd spent quite a bit of time online, learning what she could. "I feel connected to them now." Because of Kade. Because he'd drawn her into their world. "You know what I found interesting? That some of their adoptive children were from other countries or other cultures. They lost two of them in tragic accidents, though, so Robin wasn't the only child of theirs who died."

Kade's voice turned sad. "I can't even fathom it."

"Me, neither." Bridget couldn't imagine losing Cody, not now or when he grew into adulthood. "One of their adoptive children is of Native American descent. She's still alive. I saw pictures of her on the net."

"I never knew they had an Indian kid. But I haven't studied their personal lives, not like you're doing. Do you know what nation she's from?"

"Choctaw. Roy had Choctaw blood, too, from his maternal great-grandmother."

"I didn't know that, either. I should have paid as close attention to Roy as I did to his horse." Kade played absently with the end of Bridget's braid, which was draped across her shoulder. "That's pretty cool, him having Indian ancestry."

She tilted her head back to look up at him, loving the feel of his fingers in her hair. "I thought it was nice, too."

He stopped touching her, almost as if he was deliberately trying to shift focus. Then he said, "I was thinking about something, Bridget."

"What?" she asked.

"That I should leave early for Wyoming. That I should get on the road today."

She sat up and turned toward him, her heart sticking in her throat. "Why?"

"I just want to get there. But I'll wait until Cody comes home so he can see me off. I won't leave without saying goodbye to him."

"But you weren't planning on leaving until tomorrow."

"I know, but I changed my mind."

Because he was becoming restless. She could see it in his eyes. But she'd been seeing and feeling snippets of his unrest ever since they'd returned from California.

Hurt, she wanted to push him away, to tell him to leave and never come back. But she also wanted to grab him and hold him and beg him to stay.

Already she was becoming like her mother, stressing about a man she shouldn't even be with. To keep herself from showing too much emotion, she said, "Just go, if that's what you want to do."

"Now you're upset. Please don't be mad."

"It doesn't matter when you leave." She fought back tears. "Really, I don't care." On the contrary, she cared too much, and they both knew it. She was doing a terrible job of not getting emotional.

"I'm coming back, for cripes' sake."

"Are you?" she challenged him. "Or will you make an excuse to just stay on the road?" Although he'd let the rental cabin go and was staying with her for now, he kept most of his belongings in his truck. Aside from a few clothes and toiletries that he would be packing, he wasn't tied to her home.

He got off the couch and began to pace, moving back and forth in front of the fireplace. "It's just one day. That's all I'm doing. Leaving *one day* early."

It was more than that. It was his need to get away, to be free, to fight the bonds of their relationship. "So come back on time and prove me wrong."

"I will." He stopped pacing and stood in front of the fireplace, blocking Roy and Dale's picture. "I'll be back on Monday."

"Promise?"

"Yes, I promise."

She didn't believe him. In her heart of hearts, she didn't trust him to come through. But she stood, as straight and tall as she could, and walked over to him, needing to be in his arms.

He wrapped her in a big, strong hug, but it didn't make her feel any better. Either way, she feared that she was losing him. No matter how tightly he held her, she sensed that it was all just slipping away.

On Monday morning Kade was alone in a Wyoming motel room, freaking out about going home. Home? Bridget's house wasn't his home. He didn't live there.

This was home to him: being on the road, moving, traveling, going wherever he chose to go, whenever it suited him. He'd worked hard to create this kind of freedom, to earn the money and the reputation that afforded him this type of lifestyle.

Then, why was he reacting this way, on the heels of a clinic he did every year? Why was he having an anxiety attack?

Because he was afraid, he told himself. Afraid of

how close he'd gotten to Bridget, panicked that if he returned to her too soon, he would never want to leave.

He needed more time to sort out his feelings, to figure out how he was going to handle the romantic turmoil that churned in his gut. He sure as hell couldn't go on this way. He had to find a balance, an emotional center, a feeling that made sense.

At the moment, nothing was working. He didn't want to be in this lonely motel room by himself, yet he was scared to go back to Montana.

He'd promised Bridget that he would return today. And now he was sitting here, on an unmade bed, with frazzled nerves, debating what to do.

He reached for his coffee and lifted it off the nightstand. It wasn't sweet enough. He'd used most of the sugar yesterday and had forgotten to ask housekeeping for more.

Would he ever be able to think straight again? He was lucky that he'd gotten through the clinic without screwing up. But how many more jobs could he do in this state of mind?

Should he call Bridget and tell her that he couldn't come back today? Should he explain how he was feeling? Or should he go back and tell her in person?

He opted for the phone. It was a five-hour drive to Montana, and he couldn't cope with being behind the wheel, not without getting this out of his system.

Kade set the bitter coffee aside and got his phone. After he brought her number up and it started ringing, he put the device on Speaker.

He knew her schedule. She had to work later, but it was early enough that she would be home, maybe even lingering in bed before she had to get up and get ready.

She answered quickly. "Kade?"

Her voice hit him square in the stomach. She sounded soft and vulnerable, as if she was expecting him to crush her.

"Hey," he said, hating himself for what he was about to do. "I need to talk to you about something."

"What is it?" Her tone turned even more wary, more pained.

"I'm not going to make it back today. I need a few more days." To stare at the motel room walls, to worry himself sick. "I'm having a tough time sorting out how to do this."

"*This?* You mean you and me?"

He squeezed his eyes shut. "Yes."

"I knew you were going to walk away. I could feel it." She breathed, much too shakily, into the phone. "I knew it was over when you left early for Wyoming."

"It's not over." He opened his eyes and prayed for a solution. "I just need more time."

"It's over for me, Kade. I can't let you do this to me. I can't live my life waiting for you to treat our relationship with respect." Her voice broke. "You couldn't even keep one little promise."

"But don't you get it? Don't you understand? I'm afraid of the way you make me feel, Bridget. I'm afraid of how close we've become, of how much I've started to need you."

"Is that supposed to make me feel better? Don't you think I'm scared of needing you, too? But you don't see me running away."

"It's different for you. You're settled. You're where you want to be. I'm torn between being here and being there."

"Well, you don't have to be torn anymore. I'm making the decision for you. Don't come back, at least not to be with me. You can visit with Cody whenever you come to town, but you're not welcome into my bed or into my heart. And if you do anything to hurt Cody, you're out of his life, too."

The room nearly spun. Kade had just ruined everything. How could he have been so stupid? So selfish? "No, wait. Don't give up on me. I'll be back today. I'll get on the road right now." He scrambled for his jeans and shirt. He was already wearing his underwear. "I'll be there as soon as I can."

"It's too late, Kade."

"But I'm coming back. I'm keeping my promise."

"For how long? Until you panic again?"

"I won't let you down, not ever again." He would be there, forever, if that's what it took. "I don't want to lose you. Please, give me one more chance."

"I can't." She sounded on the verge of tears. "I just can't."

She ended the call without saying goodbye, and he threw on his clothes, determined to go to Montana and right the terrible wrong he'd just made.

Bridget sat shotgun in her mother's truck, sniffling through her tears. On her lap was a heap of wrinkled tissues. One minute she would be okay, and the next she would start bawling again.

"Are you sure you don't want to take the day off?" Mom asked sympathetically.

"I'm sure." Normally Bridget drove to work on her own, but she'd arranged for them to ride together this morning so she didn't have to be alone. "I can't just sit around all day. I'll go crazy."

"Did Cody catch you crying?"

She nodded. "I tried to hide it from him, but I broke down anyway. Now he's upset with Kade, too. But I told him not to be. That this was between his dad and me."

"And now Kade is on his way back?"

"Yes. But it's too late. I don't trust him not to do it again, and I need to nip it in the bud before we turn into you and Dad." Before Bridget was living every second of her life in Kade's roving shadow.

Mom braked at a stop sign and blew out a sigh. "Your dad never came rushing back to me when I got hurt or angry. He never reacted to me that way."

"So you're defending Kade?" Bridget dried her face with a clean tissue. "Taking his side?"

"Goodness, no." Mom took her foot off the brake and drove through the intersection. "I'm just saying that he's different from your dad in that regard. If I would have told your dad to stay away, he would have been glad to keep his distance."

"It sure sounds as though you're defending Kade." Her mother, of all people. Bridget needed support, not someone messing with her mind. "Thanks a lot."

"I'm just saying that Kade seems more sensitive to your feelings than your father was to mine."

Again, it sounded as if she giving Kade the benefit of the doubt. "Maybe I should have driven myself to work." At least she could've wallowed in her misery alone. "Your feedback isn't helping."

"I'm sorry, sweetheart. I want to be as mad at him as you are, but I'm worried that you might be jumping the gun. That maybe Kade isn't as much like Lance as I thought."

Lance. Just hearing her father's name gave her a tight and lonely feeling. "Maybe they aren't *exactly* alike, but the similarities are still there. If I forgive Kade, and he does this again, then I'll be just like you were with Dad. The circumstances will be different, but it will hurt just as badly."

"You're right. See, now, this proves that you're stronger than I ever was. I gave in to your dad every time he crooked a finger at me."

"I know, and that's why I can't give in to Kade." Bridget gazed out the window at the country scenery going by.

"I guess I was just putting myself in your place and imagining that it was your father rushing back to me." Mom's voice went sad. "I would have given anything for him to have done that."

Thank goodness Bridget had learned from her mom's mistakes. "It doesn't mean anything, not from a man who's just going to go back out on the road." And leave her aching for his company.

"I'm glad you're not crying anymore."

She touched the corners of her eyes, and then dabbed at her runny nose. No doubt her face was swollen and red. "Can we tell everyone at work that I have a cold?" She couldn't bear for people to know the truth. "No, wait, let's say it's allergies, then they won't think I'm contagious."

"Sure. We can say that. It won't be too much of a lie since they can't catch what you have."

"I wouldn't wish this on anyone."

"What are you going to do later when Kade shows up at your door?"

"I'm going to hold my ground. I'm not going to see him or talk to him or give him a chance to try to sway me." Her wounds were too fresh; she wouldn't put herself in that position. Plus, deep down, she feared that being near him could make her weak. She needed to stay away from him. Or else she might lose her willpower.

And fall foolishly into his arms once again.

As the sun set, coloring the Montana sky, Kade sat on Bridget's porch with Cody, the boy slinging angry words at him.

"You said that you were never going to hurt my mom. But you did. You're such a liar, Dad."

"I'm sorry. I'm so sorry. I never meant to hurt her. That's why I'm here, to try to fix it. I don't want to lose your mom. I still want to be with her."

"She doesn't want to be with you. She doesn't trust you not to do it again."

Kade struggled to defend himself. "You and your mom are everything to me. But I was scared of how close I was getting to her. She's the first woman who's ever made me feel things I never expected to feel." He'd been hoping to see Bridget and plead his case, but she wouldn't come outside. "I just don't know how to reason with her."

"That's a crummy plan, Dad."

Kade winced. "It does suck, doesn't it? But if your mom refuses to talk to me, how can I make it better?"

Cody shrugged. "I don't know. But I wish you guys could be together again."

"Me, too. Somehow I have to show her what she means to me. I have to prove how much I care."

How much he cared? *No*, he thought. It went far beyond that. He loved her. Positively loved her. He couldn't deny what was happening to him. He couldn't stop the truth from twining itself around his heart.

Kade Quinn was in love with Bridget Wells.

"You okay, Dad? You look kind of weird." Cody mimicked the lovelorn expression on his father's face.

"I'm just…" Accepting the truth. Being the man he was supposed to be. Determined to get his act together, he said, "I'm going to make this work with your mom. Whatever I have to do to win her back, I'm going to do it."

Cody smiled. "I can help you, if you want. I can be your partner or something."

"That makes us sound like a couple of superheroes, like in your comic book." He pulled Cody closer to him, appreciating the boy's support. "I've been meaning to tell you that I love you. I've been waiting for the right moment, but I should've said it before now."

"That's okay. I love you, too, Dad. But you're practically squeezing me to death."

"Sorry." Kade released his hold on the child. He would have to remember not to squeeze the life out of Bridget when he told her that he loved her, too.

Yet he knew that saying those words alone wouldn't be enough to save him. He needed to do more than that.

So much more.

Chapter Fifteen

Bridget stood at the stove, fixing breakfast for Cody and herself. Nearly two weeks had passed, and she'd gotten by without seeing Kade. Well, at least not up close. He'd been coming to the house to get Cody, and sometimes she peered out the window, catching glimpses of him in his truck.

She finished scrambling the eggs and spooned them onto their plates, along with the hash browns she'd made. She poured the orange juice and looked at Cody. He was already seated at the table.

She sat down across from him. "Is your dad coming by to get you today?"

"Nope." Cody dumped a dollop of ketchup onto his eggs.

"Is he leaving for New Mexico soon?" At this point, she was unclear as to the exact date Kade intended to go.

"He was there last week. He flew out and came back

a few days later. Since it was just a meeting with a new client, he didn't have to stay for very long."

"Is he going to go back? Did they hire him?"

"Yeah. They agreed on working together."

"When?"

"I don't know, Mom."

"You don't know when your dad is leaving again?"

Cody shrugged. "No."

She squinted at her son, wondering why he was being so evasive. Surely he knew more than he was letting on. He'd been spending nearly every day with Kade, dashing off to heaven knew where. "What's going on? Are you mad at me for not communicating with your father?"

He glanced up from his plate. "You have to see him sometime."

"Actually, I don't. Not unless we need to have a discussion about you."

"Then, I think you better see him today. Because Dad and I have been working on something that's superimportant to me, and I want him to tell you about it."

She squinted again. "Why can't you tell me?"

"'Cause it needs to come from him."

Her pulse jittered. She wanted to say no. But from the look in Cody's eyes, she could see that this issue wasn't going to go away, and she couldn't very well dismiss something that her son was claiming was "superimportant" to him.

Still, she couldn't jump right in, either. "I know you want me and your dad to get back together, but I can't be with him, honey. So if you two have been hatching a plot for some sort of reconciliation—"

"Just talk to him, Mom."

Dang. Her kid was being stubborn. But could she blame him? What child wanted to be caught in the middle of his or her parents' breakup? "All right. You can invite him here this afternoon, and I'll listen to what he has to say."

"You have to go to him."

"What?"

"To Cooper Ranch, where he's been staying."

Now she was really confused. Cooper was a recreational ranch near the river. "I heard that place was closing."

"I know, but it's still open for now, and Dad is renting one of the guest cabins."

"Couldn't he have just gone back to the other cabin? Or to the motel?"

"He was at the motel at first, but then he decided to go to the ranch."

She moved the food around on her plate. She was too nervous to eat. "I guess it doesn't matter where he's staying." She sipped her orange juice, needing the sugar boost. "But why can't he just come here?"

"Because the thing we've been working on is at Cooper Ranch."

"Fine. But I'm warning you, I'm not falling for a romantic ploy. So this better be something else."

"Just trust me, Mom. I wouldn't let Dad do anything to hurt you."

Oh, goodness. He sounded so grown up. Like a twenty-year-old instead of a ten-year-old. "Then, I'll go to the ranch and talk to him."

Even if she could barely breathe. Even if she was scared about what seeing Kade was going to do to her already damaged heart.

* * *

After Cody called, saying that Bridget had agreed to the meeting, Kade hurried to get everything ready. He'd already wrapped the gift that was going to be from Cody, so at least that was done. But he needed to tend to other details, so he jumped in his truck and zoomed off.

He couldn't remember ever being this excited. Or this nervous. His plan hinged on Bridget loving him the way he loved her. Deep down, he believed that she did. But until he heard her say it, how could he be sure?

He drove to town and headed to the florist. He entered the shop with a list of flowers he wanted made into bouquets.

The woman behind the counter was about sixty, with short graying brown hair and old-style cat-eye glasses perched on the end of her nose. She wore a colorful dress decorated with a floral pattern, making her look like part of the environment of the shop.

He walked straight up to her, and she shot him a friendly smile. "You look like a man with a purpose."

Boy, was he ever. He returned her smile. "I need three different bouquets." He handed her the list.

She scanned the paper. "No problem. When do you need them?"

"Today. As soon as you can manage it." But he wasn't going to stand around in the shop and wait. He had too much else going on. "I have some other things to do, so I can leave and come back."

"Sure. We'll get them done." She glanced at the list again. "Did you choose these combinations yourself?"

He shook his head. "I got them out of a book that I ordered online." He didn't want to make any mistakes in their meanings.

"Don't worry. They're going to be lovely."

"Thank you." He couldn't tell if she knew what he was up to or if she was just making polite conversation. It depended, he supposed, on how versed in Victorian floriography she was. "I don't care what type of containers you put them in, as long as it's the right flowers."

"How about if we vary them?" She showed him a basket and two different vases. "Then each arrangement will have its own unique style."

"That's fine." He didn't know anything about designing bouquets. But he did have a picture of each type of flower in the book, so at least he'd learned to identify them.

"Do you want cards attached?"

"No. I don't need anything else."

They agreed on a time for him to come back, and he left the shop and dashed into the supermarket. He also went to a nearby liquor store. He'd made a list of alcohol and mixers, too. He'd done his research ahead of time, scouring the internet and collecting drink recipes.

Finally, he returned to the florist and picked up the flowers, which were absolutely perfect. Everything was coming together beautifully. The main bouquet with the white roses made his heart jump.

Now all he had to do was head back to the ranch and get everything set up for Bridget's arrival.

Bridget drove to Cooper Ranch, wishing she hadn't gotten sucked into this. But saying no to Cody hadn't seemed like an option. Plus, as much as she hated to admit it, she was curious about what he and his dad were up to.

She suspected that it was a romantic endeavor. That

Cody and Kade had cooked up something that was designed to renew her relationship with Kade.

It wasn't fair that Kade had gotten their son involved. It wasn't right. But she wasn't going to be angry over it, not when Cody had told her how important it was to him.

It made her sad, actually, to think that her son was trying to get his parents back together. She wanted to be with Kade, too, but not if they had such an uncertain future.

Yet here she was, on her way to see him. And she'd fussed over her appearance, too, wanting to look pretty for him. She'd chosen to wear a lace-trimmed blouse and blue jeans, along with tall brown boots. She'd left her hair long and loose, knowing he liked it that way.

She took the main road onto the property. Cooper Ranch was an exceptional facility, designed for equestrian activities, but old man Cooper had died this year, and it was rumored that his heirs were having trouble keeping the place going. Supposedly they'd made some bad business decisions and were suffering the consequences. It was only a matter of time before it closed.

Although there were other recreational ranches in the area, this one was quite a bit smaller, as well as a tad fancier—a boutique ranch of sorts, with an elegant lodge and a handful of luxurious guest cabins.

Kade was staying in the cabin closest to the lodge, and as soon as she approached it, she saw him sitting on the front porch, waiting for her.

Bridget's nerves went into high gear. He looked so damned hot in his Western clothes and low-brimmed hat.

She parked her truck, and he got to his feet and came

toward the vehicle. She hoped that he didn't hug her. She didn't know if she could take being touched by him.

He didn't do anything except say hello and thank her for coming. But still, when their eyes met, she felt woozy all over.

"So what's this about, Kade?" she asked. "What have you and Cody been up to?"

"I'm going to take you inside and show you. But before I do, I have an important question for you." He paused, and then asked, "Do you love me, Bridget?"

Oh, God. She hadn't been prepared for a conversation of this caliber. To talk about being in love with him, to admit it, even to herself, made her heart squeeze. "I don't… I mean, I…don't think I can… I just can't…"

"You can't what? Love me?"

"I can't think about it, Kade."

"But I need you to think about it." He held her gaze. "Because I'm madly, crazily, desperately in love with you."

If she hadn't been leaning against her truck, her knees might have buckled. "You're scaring me." Making her dizzy and confused. "But yes…" She took a raspy breath. "I love you, too." She remained where she was, pressed against her truck, trying to keep herself steady. "I don't know how long those feelings have been inside me. But they're definitely there." Like a lump in her chest, growing bigger by the minute.

He reached for her hand. "Then, there's nothing to be frightened of anymore."

So said the man seducing her. "What about when you leave town again? How am I supposed to cope with that?"

"I'm not leaving again. I'm staying in Flower River. I worked out a deal to buy this place."

Bridget merely stared at him. "You're going to live here and run a recreational ranch?"

"Yes, I'm going to live here. But I'm going to turn it into a breeding and training facility. It has all the amenities I'll need. I can run my clinics from here and put the out-of-towners up in the cabins. I already talked to some of my celebrity clients, including the new one in New Mexico, about transporting their horses here for me to train. Plus, a lot of them are interested in buying yearlings from me, once I start breeding and training my own horses."

She was still stunned by it all. "You're putting down roots? For real?"

"Yes, for real. I took Cody with me to look at ranches that were for sale, so that's part of what we've been doing these past few weeks. Then, after I heard about what was happening with this place, I contacted the Cooper heirs to see if we could work out a deal." He tugged her toward the cabin. "Now come inside and see what else Cody and I have been up to."

Her head was spinning, right along with her heart. They entered the cabin, and he directed her to the dining room, where a sideboard held an array of fresh fruit, gourmet cheeses and lavish desserts.

On the dining table were three stunning bouquets and a gift box wrapped with gold paper and topped with an equally shimmery bow.

"Go ahead and open the gift," he said. "It's from Cody."

She removed the wrapping and lifted the lid on the box, unveiling a petite diamond-and-emerald bracelet with gold hearts. It looked similar to the toy necklace she'd buried in the time capsule, only the gems were real.

"It's beautiful." She looked up at Kade. "But why is it from Cody?"

"Because I asked him to help me shop for jewelry for you, and that's what he chose. We got it online." He fastened it to her wrist. "Now let me explain the flowers, because those are from me." He gestured to a vase with an assortment of colorful blooms. "That one means love and passion and all sorts of sexy stuff."

Oh, my. "And what does that one mean?" Steeped in the moment, in the beauty he'd created, she motioned to the taller vase with an ensemble of white roses, forget-me-nots and other magical-looking flowers.

"That's an engagement bouquet." He removed his hat, then reached into his pocket and produced a ring.

Bridget's limbs began to shake. The man she loved was proposing to her, making a lifelong commitment.

He behaved in a highly traditional manner, getting down on one knee to pop the question. "Will you marry me? Will you become my wife?"

"Yes." *God, yes.* She accepted without hesitation. She wanted to belong to him, to be his partner for all eternity.

He stood, and they gazed lovingly at each other. "This is a princess-cut diamond," he said as he put the ring on her finger. "I chose it because you wanted to be a princess when you were little."

"It's the most perfect ring ever." Tears rushed her eyes. The diamond was surrounded by emeralds, and it shimmered, right along with her bracelet.

She leaned forward, and they kissed. Bridget felt

as if she were in the middle of a fairy tale. She was so happy, she could've burst.

When they separated, he gestured to the final bouquet. "Those flowers have a special meaning, too. They're in honor of conceiving children, with each plant representing fertility and the womb."

"Oh, my goodness." Her eyes flooded again. "You want more children?"

"Yes, absolutely. Don't you?"

"More than anything." She wrapped her arms around him. "Thank you, Kade. Thank you for loving me."

"Thank you for loving me, too. I don't know what I would have done if you'd turned me down."

She couldn't fathom not marrying him, not with all that he was offering. A home, a family, the kind of commitment that solidified their bond. "I'm so proud of Cody for doing this with you."

"He wanted to help me, and he wanted you to be surprised."

"I'm still shaking from it all."

"Then, let me fix you a drink. I got the mixings for three different concoctions, so you can have your pick."

She smiled. "Which are?"

"You can have a Blushing Bride Champagne Cocktail, a White Wedding Cosmopolitan or a Wedding Belle."

Bridget wiped away her tears, happy as they were. "That's quite a theme. Can I have one of each?"

He laughed. "Yes, but then I'll be pouring you into bed. Speaking of which, will you stay here tonight? Cody already arranged to sleep at your grandmother's house."

"Does Grandma or my mom know you were going to propose?"

"No. It was just between me and Cody. But he'll tell them now, once I contact him and let him know you accepted. Is it true that that your mom has been less critical of me? Cody said her feelings toward me haven't been as bad."

"Yes, it's true. And now she's really going to like you."

He reached for her again. "So will you stay the night?"

"Yes, of course." She wanted to spend every moment she could with him.

"I can take you on a detailed tour of the ranch later. I figured we could make the lodge into our house. It's more space than we'll need, even with the other kids we're going to have." He touched her cheek. "I can't wait for us to start our life together."

"It's already starting." This was the beginning of everything that mattered, of coming home to Kade and their son, of creating a future with them, of having more babies.

She gazed at her engagement ring, then looked into her fiancé's eyes, forever dazzled by the cowboy she loved.

* * * * *

From New York Times *bestselling author Jodi Thomas comes a sweeping new series set in a remote West Texas town—where family can be made by blood or by choice...*

RANSOM CANYON

Staten

WHEN HER OLD hall clock chimed eleven times, Staten Kirkland left Quinn O'Grady's bed. While she slept, he dressed in the shadows, watching her with only the light of the full moon. She'd given him what he needed tonight, and, as always, he felt as if he'd given her nothing.

Walking out to her porch, he studied the newly washed earth, thinking of how empty his life was except for these few hours he shared with Quinn. He'd never love her or anyone, but he wished he could do something for her. Thanks to hard work and inherited land, he was a rich man. She was making a go of her farm, but barely. He could help her if she'd let him. But he knew she'd never let him.

As he pulled on his boots, he thought of a dozen things he could do around the place. Like fixing that old tractor out in the mud or modernizing her irrigation system. The tractor had been sitting out by the road for months. If she'd accept his help, it wouldn't take him an hour to pull the old John Deere out and get the engine running again.

Only, she wouldn't accept anything from him. He knew better than to ask.

He wasn't even sure they were friends some days. Maybe they were more. Maybe less. He looked down at his palm, remembering how she'd rubbed cream on it and worried that all they had in common was loss and the need, now and then, to touch another human being.

The screen door creaked. He turned as Quinn, wrapped in an old quilt, moved out into the night.

"I didn't mean to wake you," he said as she tiptoed across the snow-dusted porch. "I need to get back. Got eighty new yearlings coming in early." He never apologized for leaving, and he wasn't now. He was simply stating facts. With the cattle rustling going on and his plan to enlarge his herd, he might have to hire more men. As always, he felt as though he needed to be on his land and on alert.

She nodded and moved to stand in front of him.

Staten waited. They never touched after they made love. He usually left without a word, but tonight she obviously had something she wanted to say.

Another thing he probably did wrong, he thought. He never complimented her, never kissed her on the mouth, never said any words after he touched her. If she didn't make little sounds of pleasure now and then, he wouldn't have been sure he satisfied her.

Now, standing so close to her, he felt more a stranger than a lover. He knew the smell of her skin, but he had no idea what she was thinking most of the time. She knew quilting and how to make soap from her lavender. She played the piano like an angel and didn't even own a TV. He knew ranching and watched from his recliner every game the Dallas Cowboys played.

If they ever spent over an hour talking they'd probably figure out they had nothing in common. He'd played every sport in high school, and she'd played in both the orchestra and the band. He'd collected most of his college hours online, and she'd gone all the way to New York to school. But, they'd loved the same person. Amalah had been Quinn's best friend and his one love. Only, they rarely talked about how they felt. Not anymore. Not ever really. It was too painful, he guessed, for both of them.

Tonight the air was so still, moisture hung like invisible lace. She looked to be closer to her twenties than her forties. Quinn had her own quiet kind of beauty. She always had, and he guessed she still would even when she was old.

To his surprise, she leaned in and kissed his mouth.

He watched her. "You want more?" he finally asked, figuring it was probably the dumbest thing to say to a naked woman standing two inches away from him. He had no idea what *more* would be. They always had sex once, if they had it at all, when he knocked on her door. Sometimes neither made the first move, and they just cuddled on the couch and held each other. Quinn wasn't a passionate woman. What they did was just satisfying a need that they both had now and then.

She kissed him again without saying a word. When her cheek brushed against his stubbled chin, it was wet and tasted newborn like the rain.

Slowly, Staten moved his hands under her blanket and circled her warm body, then he pulled her closer and kissed her fully like he hadn't kissed a woman since his wife died.

Her lips were soft and inviting. When he opened her mouth and invaded, it felt far more intimate than anything they had ever done, but he didn't stop. She wanted this from him, and he had no intention of denying her. No one would ever know that she was the thread that kept him together some days.

When he finally broke the kiss, Quinn was out of breath. She pressed her forehead against his jaw and he waited.

"From now on," she whispered so low he felt her words more than heard them, "when you come to see me, I need you to kiss me goodbye before you go. If I'm asleep, wake me. You don't have to say a word, but you have to kiss me."

She'd never asked him for anything. He had no intention of saying no. His hand spread across the small of her back and pulled her hard against him. "I won't forget if that's what you want." He could feel her heart pounding and knew her asking had not come easy.

She nodded. "It's what I want."

He brushed his lips over hers, loving the way she sighed as if wanting more before she pulled away.

"Good night," she said as though rationing pleasure. Stepping inside, she closed the screen door between them.

Raking his hair back, he put on his hat as he watched her fade into the shadows. The need to return was already building in him. "I'll be back Friday night if it's all right. It'll be late, I've got to visit with my grandmother and do her list of chores before I'll be free. If you like, I could bring barbecue for supper?" He felt as if he was rambling, but something needed to be said, and he had no idea what.

"And vegetables," she suggested.

He nodded. She wanted a meal, not just the meat. "I'll have them toss in sweet potato fries and okra."

She held the blanket tight as if he might see her body. She didn't meet his eyes when he added, "I enjoyed kissing you, Quinn. I look forward to doing so again."

With her head down, she nodded as she vanished into the darkness without a word.

He walked off the porch, deciding if he lived to be a hundred he'd never understand Quinn. As far as he knew, she'd never had a boyfriend when they were in school. And his wife had never told him about Quinn dating anyone special when she went to New York to that fancy music school. Now, in her forties, she'd never had a date, much less a lover that he knew of. But she hadn't been a virgin when they'd made love the first time.

Asking her about her love life seemed far too personal a question.

Climbing in his truck he forced his thoughts toward problems at the ranch. He needed to hire men; they'd lost three cattle to rustlers this month. As he planned the coming day, Staten did what he always did: he pushed Quinn to a corner of his mind, where she'd wait until he saw her again.

As he passed through the little town of Crossroads, all the businesses were closed up tight except for a gas station that stayed open twenty-four hours to handle the few travelers needing to refuel or brave enough to sample their food.

A quarter mile past the one main street of Crossroads, his truck lights flashed across four teenagers walking along the road between the Catholic church and the gas station.

Three boys and a girl. Fifteen or sixteen, Staten guessed.

For a moment the memory of Randall came to mind. He'd been about their age when he'd crashed, and he'd worn the same type of blue-and-white letter jacket that two of the boys wore tonight.

Staten slowed as he passed them. "You kids need a ride?" The lights were still on at the church, and a few cars were in the parking lot. Saturday night, Staten remembered. Members of 4-H would probably be working in the basement on projects.

One kid waved. A tall Hispanic boy named Lucas whom he thought was the oldest son of the head wrangler on the Collins Ranch. Reyes was his last name, and Staten remembered the boy being one of a dozen young kids who were often hired part-time at the ranch.

Staten had heard the kid was almost as good a wrangler as his father. The magic of working with horses must have been passed down from father to son, along with the height. Young Reyes might be lean but, thanks to working, he would be in better shape than either of the football boys. When Lucas Reyes finished high school, he'd have no trouble hiring on at any of the big ranches, including the Double K.

"No, we're fine, Mr. Kirkland," the Reyes boy said politely. "We're just walking down to the station for a Coke. Reid Collins's brother is picking us up soon."

"No crime in that, mister," a redheaded kid in a letter jacket answered. His words came fast and clipped, reminding Staten of how his son had sounded.

Volume from a boy trying to prove he was a man, Staten thought.

He couldn't see the faces of the two boys with letter jackets, but the girl kept her head up. "We've been working on a project for the fair," she answered politely. "I'm Lauren Brigman, Mr. Kirkland."

Staten nodded. *Sheriff Brigman's daughter, I remember you.* She knew enough to be polite, but it was none of his business. "Good evening, Lauren," he said. "Nice to see you again. Good luck with the project."

When he pulled away, he shook his head. Normally, he wouldn't have bothered to stop. At this rate he'd turn into a nosy old man by forty-five. It didn't seem that long ago that he and Amalah used to walk up to the gas station after meetings at the church.

Hell, maybe Quinn asking to kiss him had rattled him more than he'd thought. He needed to get his head straight. She was just a friend. A woman he turned to when the storms came. Nothing more. That was the way they both wanted it.

Until he made it back to her porch next Friday night, he had a truckload of trouble at the ranch to worry about.

Lauren

A MIDNIGHT MOON blinked its way between storm clouds as Lauren Brigman cleaned the mud off her shoes. The guys had gone inside the gas station for Cokes. She didn't really want anything to drink, but it was either walk over with the others after working on their fair projects or stay back at the church and talk to Mrs. Patterson.

Somewhere Mrs. Patterson had gotten the idea that since Lauren didn't have a mother around, she should take every opportunity to have a "girl talk" with the sheriff's daughter.

Lauren wanted to tell the old woman that she had known all the facts of life by the age of seven, and she really did not need a buddy to share her teenage years with.

Reid Collins walked out from the gas station first with a can of Coke in each hand. "I bought you one even though you said you didn't want anything to drink," he announced as he neared. "Want to lean on me while you clean your shoes?"

Lauren rolled her eyes. Since he'd grown a few inches and started working out, Reid thought he was God's gift to girls.

"Why?" she asked as she tossed the stick. "I have a brick wall to lean on. And don't get any ideas we're on a date, Reid, just because I walked over here with you."

"I don't date sophomores," he snapped. "I'm on first string, you know. I could probably date any senior I want to. Besides, you're like a little sister, Lauren. We've known each other since you were in the first grade."

She thought of mentioning that playing first string on a football team that only had forty players total, including the coaches and water boy, wasn't any great accomplishment, but arguing with Reid would rot her brain. He'd been born rich, and he'd thought he knew everything since he'd cleared the birth canal. She feared his disease was terminal.

"If you're cold, I'll let you wear my football jacket." When she didn't comment, he bragged, "I had to reorder a bigger size after a month of working out."

She hated to, but if she didn't compliment him soon, he'd never stop begging. "You look great in the jacket, Reid. Half the seniors on the team aren't as big as you." There was nothing wrong with Reid from the neck down. In a few years he'd be a knockout with the Collins good looks and trademark rusty hair, not quite brown, not quite red. But he still wouldn't interest her.

"So, when I get my driver's license next month, do you want to take a ride?"

Lauren laughed. "You've been asking that since I was in the third grade and you got your first bike. The answer is still no. We're friends, Reid. We'll always be friends, I'm guessing."

He smiled a smile that looked as if he'd been practicing. "I know, Lauren, but I keep wanting to give you a chance now and then. You know, some guys don't want to date the sheriff's daughter, and I hate to point it out, babe, but if you don't fill out some, it's going to be bad news in college." He had the nerve to point at her chest. "From the looks of it, I seem to be the only one he'll let stand beside you, and that's just because our dads are friends."

She grinned. Reid was spoiled and conceited and self-centered, but she was right, they'd probably always be friends. Her dad was the sheriff, and his was the mayor of Crossroads, even though he lived five miles from town on one of the first ranches established near Ransom Canyon.

Tim O'Grady, Reid's eternal shadow, walked out of the station with a huge frozen drink. The clear cup showed off its red-and-yellow layers of cherry-and-pineapple-flavored sugar.

Where Reid was balanced in his build, Tim was lanky, disjointed. He seemed to be made of mismatched parts. His arms were too long. His feet seemed too big, and his wired smile barely fit in his mouth. When he took a deep draw on his drink, he staggered and held his forehead from the brain freeze.

Lucas Reyes was the last of their small group to come outside. Lucas hadn't bought anything, but he evidently was avoiding standing with her. She'd known Lucas Reyes for a few years, maybe longer, but he never talked to her. Like Reid and Tim, he was a year ahead of her, but since he rarely talked, she usually only noticed him as a background person in her world.

Unlike them, Lucas didn't have a family name following him around opening doors for a hundred miles.

Reid repeated the plan. "My brother said he'd drop Sharon off and be back for us. But if they get busy doing their thing it could be an hour. We might as well walk back and sit on the church steps."

"We could start walking toward home," Lauren suggested as she pulled a tiny flashlight from her key chain. The canyon lake wasn't more than a mile. If they walked they wouldn't be so cold. She could probably be home before Reid's dumb brother could get his lips off Sharon. If rumors were true, Sharon had very kissable lips, among other body parts.

"Better than standing around here," Reid said as Tim kicked mud toward the building. "I'd rather be walking than sitting. Plus, if we go back to the church, Mrs. Patterson will probably come out to keep us company."

Without a vote, they started walking.

Within a few yards, Reid and Tim had fallen behind and were lighting up a smoke. To her surprise, Lucas stayed beside her.

"You don't smoke?" she asked, not really expecting him to answer.

"No, can't afford the habit," he said, surprising her. "I've got plans, and they don't include lung cancer."

Maybe the dark night made it easier to talk, or maybe Lauren didn't want to feel so alone in the shadows. "I was starting to think you were a mute. We've had a few classes together, and you've never said a word. Even tonight you were the only one who didn't talk about your project."

Lucas shrugged. "Didn't see the point. I'm just entering for the prize money, not trying to save the world or build a better tomorrow."

"Hey, you two deadbeats up there!" Reid yelled. "I got an idea."

Lauren didn't want the conversation with Lucas to end, but if she ignored Reid he'd just get louder. "What?"

Reid ran up between them and put an arm over both her and Lucas's shoulders. "How about we break into the Gypsy House? I hear it's haunted by Gypsies who died a hundred years ago."

Tim caught up to them. As always, he agreed with Reid. "Look over there in the trees. The place is just waiting for us. Heard if you rattle a Gypsy's bones, the dead will speak to you." Tim's eyes glowed in the moonlight. "I had a cousin once who said he heard voices in that old place, and no one was there but him."

"This is not a good idea." Lauren tried to back away, but Reid held her shoulder tight.

"Come on, Lauren, for once in your life, do something that's not safe. No one's lived in the old place for years. How much trouble can we get into?"

"It's just a rotting old house," Lucas said so low no one heard but Lauren. "There's probably rats or rotten floors. It's an accident waiting to happen. How about you come back in the daylight, Reid, if you really want to explore the place?"

"We're all going, now," Reid announced as he shoved Lauren off the road and into the trees that blocked the view of the old homestead from passing cars. "Think of the story we'll have to tell everyone Monday. We will have explored a haunted house and lived to tell the tale."

Reason told her to protest more strongly, but at fifteen, reason wasn't as intense as the possibility of an adventure. Just once, she'd have a story to tell. Just this once…her father wouldn't find out.

They rattled across the rotting porch steps fighting tumbleweeds that stood like flimsy guards around the place. The door was locked and boarded up. The smell of decay hung in the foggy air, and a tree branch scraped against one side of the house as if whispering for them to stay back.

The old place didn't look like much. It might have been the remains of an early settlement, built solid to face the winters with no style or charm. Odds were, Gypsies never even lived in it. It appeared to be a half dugout with a second floor built on years later. The first floor was planted down into the earth a few feet, so the second floor windows were just above their heads, giving the place the look of a house that had been stepped on by a giant.

Everyone called it the Gypsy House because a group of hippies had squatted there in the Seventies. No one remembered when the hippies had moved on, or who owned the house now, but somewhere in its past a family named Stanley must have lived there because old-timers called it the Stanley house.

"I heard devil worshippers lived here years ago." Tim began making scary movie soundtrack noises. "Body parts are probably scattered in the basement. They say once Satan moves in, only the blood of a virgin will wash the place clean."

Reid's laughter sounded nervous. "That leaves me out."

Tim jabbed his friend. "You wish. I say you'll be the first to scream."

"Shut up, Tim." Reid's uneasy voice echoed in the night. "You're freaking me out. Besides, there is no basement. It's just a half dugout built into the ground, so we'll find no buried bodies."

Lauren screamed as Reid kicked a low window in, and all the guys laughed.

"You go first, Lucas," Reid ordered. "I'll stand guard."

To Lauren's surprise, Lucas slipped into the space. His feet hit the ground with a thud somewhere in the blackness.

"You next, Tim," Reid announced as if he were the commander.

"Nope. I'll go after you." All Tim's laughter had disappeared. Apparently he'd frightened himself.

"I'll go." Lauren suddenly wanted this entire adventure to be over with. With her luck, animals were wintering in the old place.

"I'll help you down." Reid lowered her into the window space.

As she moved through total darkness, her feet wouldn't quite touch the bottom. For a moment she just hung, afraid to tell Reid to drop her.

Then, she felt Lucas's hands at her waist. Slowly he took her weight.

"I'm in," she called back to Reid. He let her hands go, and she dropped against Lucas.

"You all right?" Lucas whispered near her hair.

"This was a dumb idea."

She could feel him breathing as Reid finally landed, cussing the darkness. For a moment it seemed all right for Lucas to stay close; then in a blink, he was gone from her side.

Now the tiny flashlight offered Lauren some much-needed light. The house was empty except for an old wire bed frame and a few broken stools. With Reid in the lead, they moved up rickety stairs to the second floor, where shadowy light came from big dirty windows.

Tim hesitated when the floorboards began to rock as if the entire second story were on some kind of seesaw. He backed down the steps a few feet, letting the others go first. "I don't know if this second story will hold us all." Fear rattled in his voice.

Reid laughed and teased Tim as he stomped across the second floor, making the entire room buck and pitch. "Come on up, Tim. This place is better than a fun house."

Stepping hesitantly on the upstairs floor, Lauren felt Lucas just behind her and knew he was watching over her.

Tim dropped down a few more steps, not wanting to even try.

Lucas backed against the wall between the windows, his hand still brushing Lauren's waist to keep her steady as Reid jumped to make the floor shake. The whole house seemed to moan in pain, like a hundred-year-old man standing up one arthritic joint at a time.

When Reid yelled for Tim to join them, Tim started back up the broken stairs, just before the second floor buckled and crumbled. Tim dropped out of sight as rotten lumber pinned him halfway between floors.

His scream of pain ended Reid's laughter.

In a blink, dust and boards flew as pieces of the roof rained down on them and the second floor vanished below them, board by rotting board.

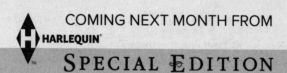

REQUEST YOUR FREE BOOKS!
2 FREE NOVELS PLUS 2 FREE GIFTS!

⊞ HARLEQUIN®

SPECIAL EDITION
Life, Love & Family

"I got past it."

"That doesn't make it right." At his chuckle, she chided, "It's nothing to joke about, Quinn."

He shrugged. "Tell me something."

She had that odd feeling again; there was more going on here than she was picking up. "Of course."

He let go of her hand, reached for his coffee—and said just what she'd been thinking. "Do you have any clue why I'm laying all this on you?"

She watched him take a sip. "Whatever your reasons, I have to say it's really nice to have a guy just sit right down and talk to me about the toughest things. It's rare."

"Right." He set the cup down again and rolled one of his unbuttoned cuffs to the elbow. "It's what women love. A guy who won't shut up…"

"I don't know about 'women.' But I know what *I* like. And you telling me about what matters to you, about what made you who you are? I do like that. A lot."

"Well, all right." He rolled the other cuff. She watched him, admiring the hard shape of his arms, thick with muscle, roped with tendons, dusted with light brown hair, nicked here and there with small white ridges of scar tissue. He went on, "But I do have a reason for loading you up with way more info than you asked for."

"And I keep trying to make you see that you don't *need* a reason."

He slanted her a teasing look. "Got that."

A low laugh escaped her. "Well, okay, then. I get it. You're trying to tell me the reason—so go ahead. I'm ready for it."

"You sure?"

She groaned and executed a major eye roll. "Will you *please* stop teasing me?"

Now he looked at her so steadily, a look that made her warm all over, especially down in the center of her. "All right." And then, just like that, he said, "I want to marry you, Chloe."

Don't miss
THE GOOD GIRL'S SECOND CHANCE
by New York Times *bestselling author*
Christine Rimmer, available October 2015 wherever
Harlequin® Special Edition books and ebooks are sold.

www.Harlequin.com

HSEEXP0915

HARLEQUIN®

SPECIAL EDITION

Life, Love and Family

Sit, Stay…Fall In Love?

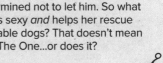

After a traumatic childhood, vet tech Jillian Everett has finally found a home in Paradise Isle, Florida. But when hotelier Nic Caruso threatens to destroy her community, Jillian is determined not to let him. So what if he's sexy *and* helps her rescue adorable dogs? That doesn't mean he's The One…or does it?

✂

SAVE $1.00

on the purchase of THE PUPPY PROPOSAL by Katie Meyer {available Sept. 15, 2015} or any other Harlequin® Special Edition book.

Redeemable at participating outlets in the U.S. and Canada only. Not redeemable at Barnes & Noble stores. Limit one coupon per customer.

52612868

5 65373 00076 2 (8100)0 12080

COUPON EXPIRES DEC. 15, 2015

Available wherever books are sold, including most bookstores, supermarkets, drugstores and discount stores.

www.Harlequin.com